MW01437060

Terraform Earth

By C.E. Chester

Lee Ann

Give me your hand, and I'll take you on a stroll through my imagination.

C.E. Chester

Publisher's Note:

This is a work of fiction. All names, characters, places, and events are the work of the author's imagination.

Any resemblance to real persons, places, or events is coincidental.

Solstice Publishing - http://www.solsticeempire.com/

In memory of Ted Lantz Sr. and all the nights we spent next to the campfire staring at the stars discussing the infinite possibilities in the universe.

Chapter One

Alhia stared at the string of amino acids on the screen in front of him, shocked that he had finally found the gene he was looking for. He rubbed his eyes, and looked at it again. Then he went up and down the chain three more times, memorizing every part as he confirmed his discovery. It was the gene that allowed a placenta to attach to the uterine wall. With this gene he could, theoretically, attach a foreign body onto a cell. He shook with the excitement of what this could mean.

A buzzing sound registered in the back of his mind. When it didn't go away, he finally looked up to see what was making the noise. There wasn't anyone at the door, but there was a flashing light next to it. It was the timer he had set to remind him of the meeting he had to attend. It had been ringing for some time, which meant he was late. After dropping what he was doing, the scientist spun around in a circle. He didn't see anything else that required his immediate attention. So, he headed for the exit, turning off the alarm before swimming into the passage way.

He tucked both arms against his torso, pressed his legs together, and fanned his feet out behind him. All of his joints flexed forward and backwards, allowing him to easily glide through the water. He turned right and headed up the spiraling corridor. Each loop was a little bit larger than the one below it. He had been on the ship for so long that he knew what tier he was on by how tight of an arc he swam.

The corridor had rounded corners and was the dark blue color water took on at depth. It gave the illusion of being in the open instead of trapped within bulkheads. The enlisted berthing was the only thing behind him, which was the largest portion of the crew. His lab was in the area designated for the civilian scientists, with their quarters close by. Above that was the officers' staterooms circling the common areas.

Hatches were kept open, otherwise the water would become stale inside the enclosed space. The few that were sealed were either not used or just shut for a moment's privacy. Alhia never paid enough attention to know which ones were closed most of the time. He had more important things to think about.

There was a shadow blocking the light filtering out of a stateroom. He was so preoccupied; it didn't dawn on him that it was an officer in the doorway until the last minute. He had to shimmy to the side to keep from hitting him. He was annoyed that someone would loiter about. Having to avoid the crewman had cost him precious seconds.

He gulped down water, and jetted it from his upper extremities at his sides. He could feel the blast wave down his legs. The sudden speed launched him around the next bend. An enlisted female stepped out of the galley, right in front of him. He veered to the left and she sprawled all of her extremities out to stop her forward moment. They just missed each other, so he continued on at the same speed. He didn't have time for apologies.

Finally, he could see the edge of the transition pool that separated the submerged portion of the Catenata from the rest of the ship above water. It was a place where they all took the time to ease their bodies into breathing air and supporting their weight. The far edge of the pool was clear. Alhia let his forward momentum propel him out of the water, caught the rim with his hands and spun around into a seated position. Water splashed up onto the wall behind him, then ran back down in rivulets around him.

Miliaris sat on the far edge. She lowered her face a quarter of the way down with a slight tilt to the left. It was a cordial greeting. Her grin made it friendly. Alhia repeated the gesture back with a neutral expression. Smiling was not something he had spent a lot of time practicing, and he worried that if he started now, it would look strange.

Her pigmentation was blue, a color found to be appealing by his race, unlike his own grey mantle. With both her arms twisted above her head, she leaned to either side. Then she placed her hands flat on the surface she sat on, arms and back straight, and took a deep breath.

She didn't speak, which was a relief. Alhia didn't like making small talk and only did so when others initiated it. When others didn't bother talking to him, he could get right to what he needed to do. He sealed his gills and took in a large breath of the humid air. It always felt weird to inflate his air sacs when he first came out of the water. His skin stretched over his expanded body. For the first couple breaths, he had to force the air back out of his mouth.

Across from him, the microbiologist stood up, continuing to stretch her lower extremities. Conscientious she might think he was staring at her, he diverted his eyes to the water's surface. Then he raised both arms up over his head, and stretched his spine to each side. Then with his arms in front of him, he twisted back and forth. His routine was to start at the top and work his way down.

Miliaris finished her stretching and went on to the meeting. Alhia knew he no longer needed to rush; she would report he was on his way. He spent the most time on his legs, preparing them for the weight they had to bear. He flexed each joint and stretched the ligaments. He loosened up the long muscles, ensuring they had good circulation. When exhaling felt normal, he slowly got to his feet. He stood there long enough to ensure he didn't have vertigo.

This area seemed like a completely different ship. The hallways were level, and walls were light grey. There were sharp angles in every corner. The filtered light from the ceiling panels was the only concession to one's comfort. From where he stood, he had two options. He could turn around and take the hall behind him, or he could skirt the pool's edge and go the way he was facing. It really didn't matter, since they both circled around to the same destination, though he would get there faster if he followed the other scientist.

Soon the sound of lapping water faded away as he made his way away from the pool. There was a hatch to his right that led to the engine room. It was always kept sealed, unless someone was going in or out. The components in that area were the only ones that could be damaged by water, so every safeguard was in place to ensure it did not flood. He had only been in there once, during his orientation on the Catenata. He remembered it being filled with large moving parts and noise. He was grateful he never had to return to it.

On his left were the shuttles used to fly around the planet's surface. This part of the ship was familiar to him, since he frequently had to go out and collect samples. The only time these hatches were closed was when there was no shuttle docked on the other side. All the doors he passed were open.

Finally, he came to a ladder that led to the space above the engine room. Being difficult to get to, it was the perfect place to put the bridge; an area only used during space travel. He set his foot on the bottom rung, and pushed up. His leg muscles protested the uncommon movement. He was grateful for the handrails on each side so he could pull as well as push himself up to the top tier. The ladder was normally only used under zero gravity, when the handrails were all that were needed to guide you in the right direction.

Usually, when a ship arrived at a planet, the crew scattered to the far reaches of it, rarely coming back to the ship. Nothing on this trip had gone as expected. Instead of exploring the vast oceans, they were still all trapped in the tight quarters used to traverse space. Because of this, they had to be creative in finding a place for their annual meeting.

He stopped at the top of the steps to catch his breath. His eyes immediately rose to the highest point of the conical ceiling, then back down the spherical beams supporting it. The room in front of him was round, ringed with display screens. They had been turned on, probably for illumination. Most the of screens showed the same thing; blue sky with water swashing against the bottom edge. Two monitors showed islands in the distance. Each display showed whatever was on that side of the ship.

In the center of the room was a large flat surface, that when powered up was the navigation array. Around the perimeter were various workstations needed to propel the ship through space. Since this area was only used during interplanetary travel when there was no gravity, there was no need for seats, which would have been nice during the meeting.

As expected, the meeting was already started. The commanding officer, Captain Yosheia, sat in the center of the room on the only raised flat surface available. He had six golden bands on his upper extremities; which meant 'captain' wasn't just a title because he was in command of the ship, but his rank as well.

At the beginning of their time on this planet, the annual meeting had dozens of scientists, many of whom had dark coloration that came with age. Now, the only researchers left, other than himself, were the three with light hues scattered around the room. It made him feel older than he was. He stepped to the steering console and sat down with the post at his back and his legs out in front of him.

"Today marks ninety-five local solar cycles we have been on this planet. We only have five more until the Commandant comes to assess our terraforming process.

What am I supposed to say when he gets here?" The Captain paused, almost as if he expected someone to answer him. Only his eyes were locked on the floor, not looking around the room. No one answered him, following his physical communications rather than his verbal ones. "We were supposed to change the planet to suit our needs, but we are the only ones that have changed.

"This planet was rated as ideal, with water covering seventy percent of its surface and all its oceans connected. We should be swimming from pole to pole and dominating all other life forms that have managed to evolve here. Instead, we are trapped in an isolated sea, and I lose one of my crew members every time we send an expedition out.

"This place was preselected," The CO continued. "Biologically-engineered animals were placed here in preparation for our arrival. With their size and intelligence, they should have taken over the oceans. But it seems they prefer living alongside the less-developed life forms. In the dozens of planets we've moved to, I've not seen a single case similar to this. The damn sea cows don't even produce milk for us. I'll be the laughing stock when word gets out that I've had my crew living on algae for a century on this forsaken place." Yosheia finally looked up at his crew. Deep lines creased his face that had been smooth when they had arrived.

For years, the subject of their lack of success had been talked about all over the ship, but never in an official meeting. Alhia looked around to see everyone's reaction. He did not want to believe the mission could be classified as a failure. It seemed the others were just as surprised as he was. Lyblepis sat against the bulkhead with his mouth hung open. The other two seemed just as shocked, though their mouths remained closed.

The silence was broken by Miliaris, with her smiling face upturned. "We've been able to secure this sea. The bio net blocks the one gap between the continent to the north of us and the one to the south, keeping this area free of predators. I don't think we will be considered completely unprosperous."

Her optimism was not shared by any of the other scientists, which was apparent by the looks she got—not that she noticed.

"Do you really think that when they get here from our home planet, completely covered in swimmable water, they are really going to be impressed with our puddle?" Ferox asked, his arms across his chest. He had just graduated weeks before the mission started and was the youngest of the civilians. He should have been in the lab cleaning up after the others, not attending a bureaucratic meeting. "I can't imagine how they are going to react to our restrictions, like not going out alone. After ninety-five of this planet's rotations, we've gotten used to things others would find horrendous. We've done what we had to in order to survive, but no one outside this group would ever look upon our situation as favorable. I have no doubt we are the last intelligent life forms this planet will ever see."

Miliaris huffed in response. She looked as though she was about to argue, but stopped when she saw the other's reactions. Lyblepis, the more senior biologist, nodded in agreement with what Ferox said. She gathered her thoughts.

"I don't think long-term habitation will be possible, but couldn't the area of this planet we've been able to secure be used as a rest stop?"

Yosheia shook his head. "I don't think that would be possible without a source of protein. One of the major perks of stopping space travel is getting to eat more than just algae."

The algae they brought to the planet with them was specifically engineered to cover all their dietary needs, including the ten amino acids their body was not able to manufacture. The room fell silent. It seemed no one else want to volunteer up any ideas that would just be shot down. Everyone looked around, waiting to see who would be the next to talk.

"Is there any progress with the biologically-engineered mammals that were introduced to the ocean?" The CO asked. He went down the same list of questions he asked every year, even though he knew the answers would be the same. He looked at the floor as spoke.

Lyblepis sat in the corner, and looked like he would prefer to be anywhere else. His hand gripped his bare upper arm. That department had been hit the hardest by the predators. It was the kid's first mission off his home planet, and now he was in charge of an entire division that had failed in every aspect of their job. He seemed too shell-shocked to even hear what had been said.

"No," Lyblepis finally answered. His face shifted from side to side, like he was looking for a way to dodge the question. "The conditions here are so harsh that they only produce enough milk to feed their calf. When the calf is no longer feeding, the milk dries up. Our only source of protein, other than the algae we brought, would be to eat animals."

Miliaris sat up straight. "It's taboo to eat anything with a nervous system, but it is also necessary that we don't consume any microscopic lifeforms. The symbiotic relationship we have with our flora is a delicate balance. If we ingested bacteria native to this planet, they would possibly overrun what is already in our body, causing us bowel upset and potentially worse. That is why we have the whales. They have the ability to digest tiny organisms."

Everyone still looked at the kid. His eyes went from one face to another, knowing they were waiting for him.

"You know, it's not my team's fault everything turned out so badly. When the aquatic mammals were seeded on this planet, there weren't any ice caps. Continental drift caused Antarctica to drift over the southern pole, disrupting the ocean currents, which caused it and the northern pole to freeze over. This amplified the seasonal changes the planet's oblong rotation around the sun and polar tilt create. Because of that, the whales had to start migrating to stay in ideal conditions throughout the year. Our ship is not constructed to navigate through the oceans. The system is designed to float in the center of the whales' nesting area. Since they are larger than any of the native species, they have no predators and thus give us protection as we establish our colony. Without them, we have little means of defense against sharks, eels, octopus, crocodiles, and squid."

He wasn't saying anything that everyone else didn't already know. But with frustration growing, it was good to hear it all again. In the heat of the moment, even they could be reduced to finger pointing. It was sometimes needed to remind everyone that the reasons for their defeat were out of their control.

"The council returns in five cycles to check our status. After a century of battling everything this planet can throw at us, I think I'm going to have to tell them we have failed."

Yosheia had a grave expression as he looked around the room. He looked like he still hoped someone could tell him he was wrong. Alhia was the only one not looking at the floor. Everyone else looked defeated; like they were waiting to be rescued.

"I have an idea."

The entire room turned to Alhia in surprise. He figured the astonishment wasn't at what he had said, but at the fact he had spoken at all. He'd never said a word in the ninety-four meetings before this one. He really didn't speak much outside his lab.

"I believe that with genetic recombination, I can domesticate the terrestrial mammals and increase mammary output. With restriction endonucleases to hydrolyze the

DNA at palindrome sequences, then polymerase III can anneal the strand. The restriction fragment length polymorphisms can..."

"We don't all have the same educational background." Yosheia turned to deliver his comment face on. "Do you mind using terminology we can all understand?"

This was why Alhia didn't like to speak; the crew couldn't bother to learn the scientific terms that were the cornerstone of all their research. After a deep breath, he dipped his head to the senior officer. "I might have a way to alter the native lifeforms to make them more docile and produce more milk. The animals on land are basically my only candidates, since that is the natural environment for mammals on this planet."

"On land?" Miliaris sat back in surprise with her hands over her mouth.

"I know logistics are going to be a nightmare. I will need a containment area and protection against predators. I haven't worked all of that out yet. First, I have to find out if I'm able to do genetic manipulation through lysogeny. At this point we have nothing to lose. Can I get permission to go on land and conduct the experiments?"

"I would give anything for a fresh glass of milk. Or better yet, a piece of aged cheese." Ferox rubbed his hands together. "No one told me I'd be surviving on nothing but algae for the entire duration."

The other two nodded in agreement.

"Well, I guess our decision is made." Yosheia stood up. "You have my permission to do your investigation. One thing you need to understand is that I will not assign anyone to help you. Walking on the surface is not natural, and I will not force anyone to do it. If you need assistance, you will have to find a volunteer."

Chapter Two

Alhia went down the ladder so fast, he missed the last two steps and landed hard on the deck below. The numbness and pain that rose up from his feet did not slow him down. He was running when he got to the transition pool. He pushed his forward momentum up into a dive, and then swam against the artificial current to get back down to his lab.

He was shocked that he had been given approval for his experiments. Interactions with native lifeforms were banned. He had only heard of a few rare occasions when that rule had been by passed. The command agreeing to his request so quickly was a sign of just how desperate things had become. This mission was the hardest he had experienced. The four others he had been on seemed simple in comparison. But being trapped in his quarters had given him a lot of time to look at DNA in ways he had never thought of before.

He was in the same hurry he had been in getting to the meeting, but now he was swimming against the currents. Though, this time his thoughts were not focused on the destination. Instead, his mind cataloged everything he would need to start working. He mentally saw where each item was in his lab. He tried to map out the most efficient way to get everything.

As he approached the galley entrance, he brought his thoughts back to what he was doing: swimming through the passageway. Since he was paying attention, no one came in or out. In fact, he didn't see anyone in the corridor. They were probably all out for a group swim. It would have been convenient if the meeting had not been scheduled to start until after the other had left for the swim. Then he would not have been put out by the other being in his way.

If he remembered it, he would send a memo with the recommendation to the captain for the next meeting.

He stopped at his hatch, prepared to start at the closest storage cabinet and gather his supplies. But he hadn't taken into account the clutter he had left out from the other projects he had been working on. He didn't have room to start anything new, but none of the things he had going were as important as what he was about to begin. So he rushed inside and put everything away that he wouldn't need.

Now he had a chance to see if his theory would work. Ideas that had been floating around in his head for years would finally be tested. In his mind, he could see the strands of DNA splicing together. There wouldn't be anything other than the specific genes he needed. He organized the samples he had already collected.

Motion in his peripheral vision made him look up. Lyblepis swam back and forth in front of the door, looking inside each time he passed. This behavior was strange, since no one ever came by just to visit him. He must be stopping by because of the experiments. Alhia turned towards him and got into the posture for greeting. The younger scientist still did not enter and looked unsure of what he should do.

"Come in. Come in."

The biologist paused at the door, pulled his shoulders back and finally entered. Once he was across the threshold, he stopped and still didn't speak. His eyes stayed on the deck.

"Is your teammate pressuring you to help me?" Alhia asked.

"No." Lyblepis shook his head. After a deep breath he looked up. "I cannot help you. Our department had over thirty members when we arrived here. Now it is just Ferox and myself. I know that most of our mission is a failure, but there are still a lot of things we handle. Under normal conditions, there are two or three staff members just for the day to day running of the ship. The two of us are handling that the best we can, but we are overwhelmed with the workload. I do want to help in any way I can, though. I brought you the logbooks from the senior scientist that worked with the aquatic mammals. I don't know if any of this will help you, but I brought it over just in case it might."

Lyblepis looked tired. The flesh around his eyes was sunk in. His shoulders sagged. The stress was taking its toll, but that wasn't the only contributing factor. Everyone on the ship had the same weariness. They all needed something, even something as simple as a glass of milk, to compensate them for everything they had sacrificed.

After dumping the logs onto the closest flat surface, the younger crewmember retreated without saying anything more. Even though the biology division had been hit the hardest by predators, the entire ship was shorthanded. Which meant that Alhia would be probably be doing everything by himself. Being alone didn't bother him. The thought of hard work did not discourage him, either. It was better than just waiting for the next five solar rotations to pass and the trip to be over.

Chapter Three

Alhia's eyes ached from staring at the display screen for too long. Even when he closed his eyes, he could still see chains of adenine, guanine, thymine, and cytosine. He needed to take a break and clear his mind. Going for a swim would be perfect. He longed to go out by himself, let the currents carry him away, and explore the farthest depths, but that was neither safe nor allowed. If he wanted to go for a swim, he would have track down the Officer of the Day and register to be in today's group. Then he would have to wait until the designated time, go out with everyone else, and stay in a school like he was a fish. He looked up and checked the time. It was almost dawn. He needed to find a place to conduct his experiments. Taking out a shuttle wasn't the same as swimming, but at least he'd be on his own and exploring.

Unlike him, it seemed most of the crew had adapted to the planet's day and night rotations. He blamed it on being in his lab all the time, completely locked away from the changes outside, but his body always followed its own rhythm. If he was working, he would lose track of what was going on in the world around him.

He made it to the shuttle without seeing anyone. Out of habit and training, he checked the schedule. As he expected, none of the aircraft had been reserved. Most of the missions had been cancelled, so there wasn't any reason to travel. Even though he felt silly doing it, he put in the log book that he would be taking a shuttle for the next five days. He didn't want any of the military personnel upset because he hadn't followed protocol.

He stepped through the door of the shuttle and sealed the hatch behind him. Usually his next step was to stow away his gear in the storage compartments, but he was empty-handed. In the cockpit, he went through the preflight check list. First thing was to assess the atmospheric conditions. Then he looked at every gauge to ensure the craft was operational. Everything was in order. He dialed up the throttle and hovered over the ship. From there, he had a fantastic view of the sea. The far islands that could barely be seen from the observation screens stretched out in front of him.

Based on the charts he had, he set a course due south. The initial scans of the planet when they had first arrived showed the upper part of the continent as all grasslands. With that much area to choose from, he shouldn't have any difficulties finding the place and animals he needed. As he approached the shoreline, all he could see was sand. There were no marking of scale of the images, so he wasn't sure how far inland the beach would extend.

After a few minutes, he became concerned when there was still no vegetation in sight. The dunes went as far as he could see in every direction. It was hard for him to believe there wasn't anything but dry, parched land. He turned on the long range sensors, assuming they would find the life his eyes couldn't. The screen was blank and silence was his only response. After a few minutes, he turned the equipment off in frustration.

There was something off to the west that looked different than the monotony around him. With a banking turn, he headed off in that direction. The feature proved to be farther away and larger than what he had estimated and nothing more than a mountain range. He flew to it, hoping there would something different on the other side. The view over the top was of another length of rocky peaks and the ocean beyond.

Since there was nothing ahead of him that held any potential, he turned around. While backtracking over the terrain he had already seen, he studied the charts. The image showed the mountains he had just crossed, so he was in the right place. Somehow the plant life had all disappeared.

The flight continued on much longer than he thought it would. He was out of food and had accessed the emergency rations of water to keep from getting dehydrated, but as long as there was ground beneath him, he pressed on. He could not imagine the desert extending across the entire continent.

The terrain was monotonous and boring, so when the green appeared below him, he blinked in disbelief. To his surprise and relief, the foliage was still there when he opened his eyes. There was an immense river flowing north to the sea they were anchored in. Lush plant life grew on both banks. He set the scanners to alert him if there were any animals, and was startled when the alarms went off before his hand was back on the altitude controls.

He leaned down to look at the view screen and a close up image of a group of animals standing along the embankment. He jaw dropped open. He was sure his tired eyes were playing a trick on him. He throttled back, and went into a hover for a closer look. The mammals were standing upright, on their hind legs, like him. He was confused by the assortment of different-colored fur they all had. Usually, animals in a herd were all related in one way or another and similar in appearance. Then he realized what he saw wasn't fur; it was the pelts of animals they had killed. He probably wouldn't have jumped to that conclusion if they hadn't been carrying weapons, but each of them held a long stick with a sharp rock attached to the end.

He was not aware any of the primates had evolved this far. Some of them had paint on their faces. He knew they wouldn't pose any danger for the crew, but a pack of organized hunters would pose a threat to any animals he domesticated. Most of the strange new animals cowered down with their spear tips pointed towards him, but two large males stood defiantly staring up. If they really had no fear, than it would be a waste of time even trying his experiments here. He spun the plane around and punched the throttle. He set the course to take him back to the Catenata as fast as he could get there. He had underestimated how quickly things on this planet changed. It seemed everyone had.

***

The next morning, Alhia climbed into the shuttle. His arms were full of provisions and he restocked the water he had consumed the day before. Then he stowed what he had brought for future use. When that was complete, he went through the checklist to launch. He was no longer confident he would find land suitable to browse animals on. He had decided to fly north and inspect the continent in that direction. None of the scans looked ideal, but he had already learned that things can change drastically. He needed to look for himself.

One strip of land jutted out to greet him. He adjusted course to fly over it. His first impression was that the land was too steep. Uneven terrain would make setting up a confinement system difficult and wasn't something he wanted to walk on. Beneath the surface, he saw a land riddled with volcanic activity.

The peaks continued to grow higher as he went, making him climb in elevation as they did, and eventually becoming too steep and too high for trees to grow on. He pressed on, over the top and down the other side. When he finally did find level ground, it was a frozen ice sheet that stretched as far as he could see. The glaciers had moved farther south than his scans showed. It seemed this planet's ice age wasn't in recession after all.

The project might be done before he even started. Without a place to tend the animals, there was no point with trying the genetic manipulation. He felt like an idiot for bringing up his ideas to the captain before doing this crucial step. But he had said something… in front of the other scientist.

Too frustrated to return to the Catenata, he punched the throttle and flew towards the sunset. Eventually the ocean came into sight. He thought he'd find large waves crashing against the shore, to match his mood, but small, smooth swells rolled up on the beach. At the sight of it, he took a deep breath, and then redirected his gaze out at the endless salt water in front of him. He didn't slow down until he was far enough away from the coastline for the curvature of the planet to block the sight of land. Only then, was he able to take in a full breath and slowly release it.

Alhia touched down on the water's surface. He had no intention of getting out of the craft. Swimming in the open ocean was prohibited, not that he needed someone to tell him it wasn't safe. He had seen the carnage of a shark attack first-hand. He closed his eyes, letting the waves rock him, and turned his attention to the sound of the water lapping against the hull.

He was constantly surrounded by bulkheads. His laboratory was in the center of the ship. He had a screen and could tune it to any of the camera views outside the ship, giving him the illusion of having a window, but it wasn't the same. It wasn't normal for his species to be trapped indoors. It was even unusual for them to congregate together. They would swim vast distances to find isolation.

Opening his eyes, he looked out the windshield at the open water. For the first time in longer than he could remember, he did not feel closed in. The tension in his extremities eased. His breath slowed down as he sat there peering out at the nothingness. Only a few more solar cycles and he would be able to return to a planet they had already conquered. He had to remember that even though the current conditions were horrible, there was an end in sight.

Daylight disappeared behind the horizon while he sat there thinking. In the night sky, he was able to see two other planets in the solar system, though it was seeing the Milky Way on edge high above him that finally gave him clarity. This small star with only one planet covered in water was in a distant part in the galaxy, twice as far as any other planets they had terraformed. He had signed up for the mission knowing he would travel farther than any other crew before. All they had to do was complete the timetable they had been assigned and he could return home able to say he had done something only he and the others on his ship had completed. It would be better if they had succeeded in the terraforming process, but now was not the time to examine what should have happened. It was time to appreciate what they had accomplished.

***

Alhia sat down in the cockpit for the third morning in a row. It seemed pointless, but he wasn't ready to give up. He checked the gauges, which all said the same thing they did every morning. When that was finished, he took the controls in hand and pulled into a hover.

He had already explored everything to the north and south. The only thing to the west was open water. That left him the land to the east. He hadn't even bothered looking at the scans. They all seemed too old to reveal anything about the current conditions. The only way he was going to find what he needed was to go out and search for it.

It took longer to cross the sea in this direction. Clumps of islands passed underneath him. Eventually, the far shore came into sight. He was immediately relieved to see the sand was just a small ribbon that stretched up and down the coast. He had finally found the prairie he needed. He slowed down and dropped to a lower elevation. He set up the sensors to scan for mammals underneath him. He was on the edge of his seat, trying to see everything before he flew over it.

Dots appeared on the horizon. He zoomed in and saw a herd of bovine marching through the tall grass. So not only had he found a place with the right plant life but had also found an ideal specimen for his research. Suddenly, he had hope that he might get to do his experiments. Even though this area would work, he still believed that there might be something better up ahead. He kept the speed and course heading steady. There were a variety of animal species. He photographed each species he came across. He hoped to find natural terrain that would isolate his specimens, but hadn't seen anything like that yet.

Then two rivers came into sight that paralleled each other as they flowed south, with a lush valley between them. This was the most promising prospect he had seen so far, so he turned to follow the current. There was a large mountain range to the east. He stayed between the rivers, and flew low to the ground. There were large herds scattered across the plains. He smiled with excitement of finally finding a place that held true promise. When he noticed that he startled some of the animals, he raised in altitude, but just enough to keep from disturbing them. He kept watch for predators but didn't see any as he passed.

Eventually, the two rivers joined to make one body of water. The sun was high in the sky, and he was already getting hungry. First he retrieved some algae to squelch his appetite, then he looked at the flight recording. He hadn't gone as far as he thought he had. The slower speeds to be able to see what he passed made it feel like he had gone farther than he actually had. He was still close enough to the ship to be able to make daily flights to the area.

He continued flying above the river, even though he doubted he would find anything better than what he had already seen. Then a change in the topography made him turn around to take a closer look. The river plunged over a sharp cliff. Sometime in the past, the waterfall had been miles wide, carving out a panoramic cliff face. Now the river dove over a small section of it, then flowed down the valley that had been created ages ago.

There were no animals in this area because the cliff was too steep to climb down, but green grass and small trees stretched on either side of the water. The isolated valley ended at another cliff, where the river plunging into the sea. The second cliff was high enough that salt water would not be able to flow upstream, even at high tide. Since moving the animals would not be a problem, he had found the perfect place. He didn't even need to use a bio net.

Chapter Four

Back on the Catenata, Alhia was in a rush. He had mass-reproduced the DNA chain he needed to deliver and had it in a solution. Now he needed to find a way to administer it to the mammals. He had been through every cupboard, every drawer, and every storage container in the room. He didn't feel confident that any syringes he had would make it through the thick fur and tough hides of the animals. There was only one person he could think of that would be able to help him, and unfortunately, he was on the other side of the ship.

With relief, he made it through the common area without bumping into anyone. The conversation he had to have would be taxing enough. Sometime it seemed he was the only person on the crew who remembered they were a solitary species. It was ironic that the ship's captain thought being on the surface was the worst part of the endeavor, but he felt it was the forced interactions he suddenly had to have.

He slowed down just past the galley and stopped two doors down. The first room was about the size of his lab and similar in make-up. All the walls were covered in shelves and cabinets. Everything was available for any routine visits to medical. This was a far as Alhia had ever been. The only time he had been here was to drop off his medical record when he reported to the ship.

The only one there was Velifer, the medical officer, with four golden bands on his arm. His attention was focused on a screen. Alhia waited quietly until he was done reading.

Unlike the ship's doctor, none of the scientists were in the military, commissioned or active duty. They weren't required to go to any of the military schools and wore no rank. They were contracted for each mission to do the job they had gone to school for.

One of the first things he had done was learn the basics of the rank insignias. More stripes meant higher ranking, gold bands were officers, black chevrons were engineers, and white chevrons were deck crew. Nine bands were the most anyone could achieve.

"Oh, no. Not you." The physician's exclamation brought the scientist out of his reverie.

Alhia recoiled. He assumed that was how others responded to him, but this was the first time it had been said out loud. The officer's lips curled back in a snarl, and he had his hands up in front of him.

"I cannot help you with your… experiment. None of my training can be useful with beasts. The captain declared I don't have to help you." In his agitation, Velifer's body rose in the water, leaving him looking down on the other man.

"I'm not here to employ you." The scientist held both hands out at his sides. "I'm only in need of your advice, and possibly some of your equipment. I need a way to dose the animals with my serum. I'm not confident anything in my lab will get through their thick fur and hide."

"Oh, is that all?" The doctor relaxed his posture. "Yes. Yes. I have something that should work."

The next room was larger, but had the same layout. The only difference was a horizontal surface in the center with straps attached to it. He knew it was for patients who were unable to swim. He veered closer to the cabinets, not wanting to be close to it. The doctor continued on through another series of opened hatches.

This room was smaller than the last, and had four beds with straps taking up most of it. The room looked unused, and had storage containers haphazardly laid on the would-be sleeping platforms. After digging around in a couple of bins, a long syringe, twice as long as what was normally used, was produced.

"I never use this style. Won't miss it at all."

"I'll return it as soon as I'm done." The geneticist bowed to show his gratitude.

"No need." Velifer waived and went back to the front.

He stared at the doctor's back with mixed feeling. He was glad the encounter was over. Especially this one, with Velifer's violent insistence of not helping, but part of him was curious about what had caused such strong feelings. The physician didn't seem interested in explaining anything, though, and it really didn't matter. He had everything he needed from the man, and he needed to get back to work.

***

Alhia had the serum in hand and the syringe to deliver it. Excitement had him up and flying out at the break of dawn, which also meant he was flying due east at sunrise. The automatic tinting was not enough to shield his eyes from the blinding light rays, so he changed course to fly to the southeast. It was still bright, but he could see.

It was the fifth day he had the shuttle reserved for. He hadn't flown this route before. He went over the mouth of the river he had found his first day of exploring. It was wider than he had imagined it would be. The muddy shallows reached far out into the sea. He was tempted to slow down and appreciate the view, but figured he could do that at a later date. Today, he had plans that were more urgent. Instead, he continued on the same trajectory, over a large peninsula.

At the far side was the long narrow sea he had flown over before. This was the landmark he had been looking for. He turned north, keeping his plane between the beaches. Ahead of him he could see the cliff face, and the river plunging over its edge. Since he was traveling at full speed, not like he had to inspect the area, he was over dry land before he realized it. The grassy plains with scattered trees stretched before him. The next escarpment rose higher than the treetops. Another scan confirmed there were no mammals in the vicinity, which meant there were no natural predators to worry about.

Above the second waterfall, he found multiple herds grazing. One herd had his expectations up; they looked large enough to produce the needed quantities of milk. He landed behind a clump of trees, hoping the animals would be calmer if they couldn't see the craft.

He climbed out of the pilot seat, and took a moment before he rushed off. He was a little stiff after sitting for so long, so he moved his hips front and back. He didn't know how much exertion was going to be required, so he limbered up. With arms in front of him, he twisted side to side. He bent his knees in both directions and articulated his ankles in full circles. With a deep breath, he looked at the back of the cabin and decided to was time to do what he promised he would.

He had packed everything the night before, so once he was ready to start, all he had to do was grab his bag. The ramp lowered, letting the bright sunshine in. He squinted, blinked a few times, then stepped back to stay in the shadows until his eyes adjusted. By the time his pupils had constricted, the ramp was all the way down. He stepped out into the warm solar rays. It was the ideal temperature to work in.

He took two steps, then stopped. Sound waves were strange on the surface. Underwater he felt them along his jaw bone. Out in the air, he had to rely upon his seldom-used ear canals, making it seem like the noise was not something happening to him. It took him a moment to realize it was the bottles rattling together that was ruining the silence. He climbed back into the shuttle and found something to put between them.

Now the only thing he heard was the wind rustling the leaves. He walked confidently without clatter from his pack. The ground felt cooler when he stepped into the shadow of the tree. He looked up at the flat green membranes shaking in the breeze. It seemed they were quite proficient at absorbing the light.

The terrain was flat. He stepped wide of the trunk to avoid the roots that were protruding from the soil. While making his way, he stepped on a fallen branch. The sound of the wood cracking was loud. He froze in place, and watched the animals to see how they responded. For a long time, they just stared at each other; the large hairy beasts and the smooth-skinned stranger standing upright in their field. Alhia wished he was in the water. There he would have no problems being stealthy; he would be able to do loops around these simple animals without them knowing he was there.

Slowly, a few cows at a time went back to eating. Some of them even turned their back on him in search of more grass. When only a couple still looked his way, he took another step. He only moved one foot, and then waited to see if there was a reaction. When he didn't see any distress, he took another, then another stride, carefully avoiding the twigs littering the ground. It was slow going, since he had to look down, find clear footing, then look up for any reaction.

As he stepped out from the shadow of the tree, the whole herd looked up at him. He thought it was fine. He hadn't made any noise. He was the same figure that had been walking towards them for some time. One or two had been looking up at him since he stepped on the branch. None of them seemed upset. So, he took another step with dozens of eyes still on him.

One took off, sprinting away from him. Instantly, the entire herd kicked up dust with their thundering hooves. He had no idea animals that big could run that fast. He watched in awe as they quickly faded from sight.

With a sigh, he turned around and headed back to the ship. The shuttle looked farther away then he thought it was. Apparently he had covered a lot of ground before reaching the shade, and the swath of trees suddenly seemed wider. Thankfully he no longer needed to be silent as he marched back to the plane. By the time he got there, he was out of breath.

From the air, he could see where the herd had gone off to. This time, there weren't any trees close by, so he landed twice as far away. He didn't make any noise on the dewy grass, but he understood the animals relied on their vision to assess threats just as much as their hearing. He didn't want to seem like a predator coming in for attack. He would walk a few feet, then feign interest in something else. He used optical equipment to scan the herd when he stopped.

The cattle were spread out over the field, taking a few bites, walking forward, and then eating more. Each cow went its own way without any symmetry or organization. He tried to discern a pattern in their movements, but couldn't come up with any.

Alhia came to a section of rocks without finer soil or plants between them. The stones had been heavily eroded, so there were no sharp edges to hurt him. The pebbles shifted under his feet, creating more noise than the twigs had. He closed his eyes and took a few deep breaths to remind him to stay calm and remain still. When he didn't hear a stampede, he opened his eyes to see most of the animals had already gone back to eating. Only a few kept looking at him.

Staring at the animals only distracted him. He turned his attention to the ground and switched directions to step on a rock bigger than his foot. The rock was stable and made no sound. He let out a pent-up breath he didn't realize he had been holding. He had to leap to the next rock. It was balanced above another one. When he put his weight on it, the top rock shifted, smacking into the rock below it. The clangor made the herd look at him. He had looked up to check on the animals without ensuring his own footing, lost his balance, and he fell over.

His flailing arms, trying to stop the fall, sent the animals off in another charge. With a sigh, he laid his head back on the ground. There was no need to jump up; he had no hope of catching them. When Alhia finally did stand up, he had to brush dirt and debris from his posterior. There was no sign of blood, but he was sure there would be a deep bruise on his hip.

Once again back in the air, he circled the valley until he found another species. These animals were significantly smaller than the ones he had just tried to approach. Earlier, he had dismissed them as test subjects, because each one would produce such a small amount of milk. Now, he just wanted to get his serum into an organism, so he could see if the genetic changes would take effect. If it did work, he could make more and administer it to as many species as he wanted to.

He parked near the bank of the river. The rushing water was louder than any noise he made, so he set out with hope this time would be successful. He climbed down the ramp, with one eye on the animals busily eating grass. He was able to walk confidently on the solid ground with lush vegetation.

The smaller animals were more on alert than the larger ones had been. It made sense, being that they were probably easier to bring down. Every time one would look up, he froze. He did not move again until they all looked down, which meant he was only able to take a few steps at a time.

The closer he got, the longer it took for them to go back to eating. He hadn't closed much of the distance between them, when the animals changed tactics. Instead of randomly checking between bouts of grazing, they took turns watching their surroundings. The one acting as lookout would not eat until another one looked out at the horizon. Progress became even slower when he had to wait for the animal to look the other way.

Then one flinched and the whole flock raised their heads. Alhia was tired. He didn't want to play these silly games with small-minded under-evolved organisms. The only thing that kept him locked in place was the knowledge that the test couldn't begin until the new DNA was injected. Another one flinched. Suddenly, the entire flock was running towards the trees at full speed.

Alhia stomped back to his shuttle, not caring if he made a ruckus. There was nothing left to hear him. The water rushed by as if it were mocking him. Everything he needed to do the experiments was right here at his fingertips, and he couldn't finish the first step. He turned his back on the flowing water and went up the ramp. At the top, he used the controls to raise it.

After securing his unused gear, he lowered himself into the pilot seat. His bruised and tired muscles triggered pain receptors, letting him know his body wasn't up for any more physical exertion. He exhaled a larger-than-normal breath and looked out of the front screen. The green grass swayed in the breeze, causing ripples that traveled as far as his eyes could see. This location was perfect. He was sure the test results would be positive. He felt physically beaten, but mentally he wanted to keep trying.

He launched into the air. With a few hours of daylight left, he didn't need to rush back to the Catenata. At first, he made large lazy circles, not really paying attention to anything around him. He couldn't make a decision about where to go or what to do. He was used to there always being a next, logical step. And there would be… once he delivered the serum. Until then, he was stuck flying around in loops.

Eventually he grew tired of banking to the right, and shifted the controls until he turned to the left. There was no reason for him to make the course change. It didn't bring him enlightenment or change what he looked at. The scenery was still a river, grass, and an occasional tree dotting the landscape.

Then the sensors pinged. They were still set to scan for mammals. In a field to the west of the shuttle stood the herd he had originally tried to inoculate. They were sprawled out and grazing. His hands went to the steering controls, and soon he was circling them instead of the empty plain.

He knew there had to be a way to administer the shots. He just had to think about it from another perspective. He had to open up his mind to other solutions instead of failing at the same thing over and over. Maybe if he watched the animals, he would have an epiphany? So, he leaned forward, over the controls, and focused on the cattle. He watched how they ate, how they lifted their tail when they urinated, how they slightly tilted their pelvis when they defecated, how they walked, and how they looked up. Then he realized they were all looking up at him. He had been paying so much attention to what was on the ground that he hadn't noticed how low he was flying.

He pulled back on the controls and put space between him and the herd. They put their heads back down and munched on the green stems. Another lap around and nothing had changed. They did the same thing they always did: ate, released waste material, took a few steps and ate some more. There wasn't anything to inspire an epiphany, because they didn't do anything.

Maybe that was what he needed to change? Maybe they needed their routine shook up a little? Maybe if he watched how they reacted to predators; he might gain some insight into how to keep them calm? Maybe he didn't need to keep his elevation up?

He leveled the wings to stop the turn, then leaned forward to start his descent. The cows took off running and did not stop. He went into a hover to watch them run. The herd stayed together as they headed south.

There was no need to pursue them. From the air he was able to see how they all maintained speed and direction getting away from their last known threat. They looked like a school of fish, but on land. Alhia's eyes were drawn to the horizon, and the cliff face they were speeding towards. If they didn't change direction, they would all plummet to their deaths.

He waited. Surely, they would slow down or veer off course. He didn't think it was possible for the herd to reach the numbers they had if they were stupid enough to plunge off a cliff. But to his disbelief, they kept a constant heading.

The only thing Alhia could think of to do was punch the accelerator, fly up high, and beat them to the precipice. Then he switched into a hover when he was at the edge. He turned around to see the beasts still running at him.

He was confused. His presence should deter them. The shuttle was what had spooked them in the first place, so having it in front of them now should make them change direction. Just when he was about to give up hope, the lead animal swung to the left, and led the others parallel to the edge. Exhaling with relief, he stayed in position until the last one turned.

To keep the herd in sight, he had to increase the altitude. He was impressed by their stamina. Even after all the distance they had covered, they still sustained the fast pace. Now they were all running towards the river. He saw no reason to be concerned. The water was visible and something they encountered every day.

The herd plunged one after another into the current. Their attempt at swimming seemed feeble to Alhia, since they could only use their long extremities designed to walk on land. They did stay afloat, but were quickly carried downstream. The exhaustion became apparent as they struggled to get to the other side. He could see the panic in their eyes. They were finally aware of the danger they were in. A few made it to the far side and crawled up on the bank, but they were the largest and strongest. The surging water carried the rest towards the falls.

Alhia went into action. He swooped the shuttle down and engaged the anti-gravity lift. After the fourth cow, the engine bogged down with the strain. It was illogical to risk overloading the equipment when he didn't have to take them far to get them to safety. So, he dialed up the throttle, and carried his load to the far bank. As soon as he was over land, he set the quartet down. Turning around to make another pass took valuable time. He went as fast as he could and went straight for the ones closest to the edge. On his fourth pass, he wasn't quick enough. He watched two cows fall out of sight.

There wasn't time for him to react. There were still more animals in the water. He flew in tight loops until the last one was on shore. Only then did he mash the accelerator and take off to the northeast. He skimmed along the snow-covered mountain tops, not wanting to see another creature or think about what he had just witnessed. This was the first time he had caused the death of another living organism. And even though he had saved almost all of them, he was still responsible for the ones he hadn't.

The overwhelming emotions caused him to fly erratically. Knowing he would crash if he didn't stop, he found a cleared hilltop below the snowline and landed on it. A view of the lush valley and the grass lands beyond it were laid out in front of him.

He was grateful to be alone. If anyone else knew what he had done, he would never be able to face the crew again. Their species did not believe in killing. The planet had been selected after a catastrophic event had annihilated most of its lifeforms. The engineered mammals were placed in the oceans as soon as the conditions were stable. It was the same process that had been done over and over throughout the galaxy. No other world had this explosion of life, and nowhere else had he been required to face death.

The entire crew had been traumatized. All he hoped to do was give them one small thing they could enjoy. The area had been so promising. He was sure he would succeed here. Now, he wasn't even sure if the project would continue. Then he wondered if he could stop. If he terminated the project, the others would want to know why? Would he be able to lie to them? There was no way he could let anyone know what had happened. It seemed some prevarication was required.

Eventually his breathing and heart rate returned to normal levels. Whatever option he ended up with, he would not make the decision on land. He eased the throttle open, and flew home.

Chapter Five

Alhia jerked awake, then immediately closed his eyes to hold onto the image he had thought of in his sleep. He could see it in his head, a protein envelope surrounding the DNA strand and the capsid, protecting it from environmental factors. It would have a sheath like a miniscule syringe, to push the inner tube through the host cell's wall and membrane, forming a passageway for its nucleic acid into the interior of the cell. He knew the gene for creating cell markers, it could easily be mutated to be peplomers to attach the structure to of a cell.

He rolled out of his hammock so fast that his upper extremities got caught in the fabric. With a little wrestling, he was able to get free. Air bubbles he had stirred up were carried around the room by the current. He watched them swirl as his heart rate lowered. He was grateful to already be in his lab and able to start working immediately.

Before, he had shared a berthing area with five other scientists until they all died in animal attacks. Going back into that space was a constant reminder of death. Eventually he couldn't take it and moved his hammock into the laboratory.

He was quickly able to find the gene he needed to serve as the peplomer. He heated the sample until it was just below boiling, causing the DNA to temporarily become denatured, breaking the hydrogen bonds holding the double helix together, separating it into two strands. Then he used a restriction endonuclease to clip the gene out of the polynucleotide strand at the palindromes, making a restriction fragment length polymorphism.

Once assembled, he inserted the new polypeptide into cells and watched as new virions were released by budding off a small segment of the cell wall. It was lunch by the time he looked up at the clock and well into the night before he had the quantities he needed.

He was so caught up in finding out if it was possible that he hadn't stopped to consider if he should. Did he want to fly back out there to the scene of the massacre? It was his own personal nightmare, literally what he saw every time he closed his eyes. But it was still his own private hell. No one else knew about it, and he had to keep it that way. If he suddenly stopped the tests, everyone would question him. He was prepared to make up a lie and stop it all, but that was before his great insight. Now he was sure he had to continue, since he had to keep his secret either way.

Even after working late into the night, Alhia was still too excited to sleep, but he didn't want to risk anything going wrong with the experiment. He needed to wait until daylight. Technically, he could do it all with his instruments, but then he wouldn't have anything to fall back on if anything went wrong. Waiting just a couple of hours would increase his chance of success by forty percent.

Reluctantly, he crawled back in his hammock. A few hours of rest would help him start the next phase of his test with a clear head. The letters A, T, C, and G danced around in his head. He didn't feel like he had drifted off to sleep until he woke up just in time to go back to work.

The virions were no longer in small vials. Now he had two large containers of liquid, one in each hand, that he had to carry up to the shuttle, which meant he was unable to jet water through his upper extremities. Add to that the fact that he was basically carrying an anchor in each hand and it made very slow going to the transition pool. He lifted them out of the water, one at a time, and then hoisted himself onto the ledge next to them.

The terminal flashed for him to check in for his flight. Since he hadn't been sure if he was going to continue with the experiment, he hadn't reserved any aircraft. If this terraforming process had gone as expected, he might not be able to get a shuttle. Of course, if the mission had gone how it was supposed to, then he wouldn't be doing the experiments. He let out an exasperated sigh and walked over to the monitor. He confirmed that he would need one plane for the entire day. When asked if wanted to reserve it for future dates, he replied yes. He scrolled down through the list of options, and was surprised to see 'daily until mission is complete' at the bottom of the list. He selected that and was relieved to know he would never have to bother stopping at the terminal again.

Through the windshield, he could see the sky was still dark. He glanced up at the familiar constellations before starting his preflight routine. The sky had always been a source of wonder and amazement for him, one of the main reasons he kept signing up for missions. He was always curious about what the next solar system looked like. What twists and turns would the double helix make on the next planet? Now he was in a position to not just observe and catalog the natural mutations, but to generate a few of his own.

With renewed excitement, he took off. The flight seemed much slower than all the others had been, even though the gauges indicated he was traveling at maximum speed. He passed the time by watching the darkness fade below him. Shadows emerged underneath trees, then the colors appeared. As he slowed to hover over the river, the first rays of sunlight broke over the mountains.

Alhia laughed when he saw the valley filled with fog. He had worried it would be too simple to just rain the solution down on the herd. Going airborne didn't seem absurd with so many water particles already suspended in the air. The mist was so thick, he couldn't see the animals in the field. He had to rely on his scanners to know where they were. He flew in a grid pattern, spraying his solution until the tank was dry.

By the time he was done, the warm sunlight was breaking up the fog. He flew south, past the falls, to the open expanse below them. He was glad he did; the two carcasses of the cows that had been swept over the edge had washed up on the shore of the river below. He couldn't leave them there. First off, if anyone from his crew saw them, they would be horrified. But more importantly, the rotting meat was already starting to stink. There were no scavengers in the area, but he had no doubt they would soon be looking for a way down the cliff if they knew there was a guaranteed meal at the bottom.

He used the lift to pick them up. Not knowing what else to do, he continued south until he was flying over the narrow sea. He dropped the load, feeling it was ironic he was feeding the fish that had made his life miserable.

Chapter Six

The daily flights out to check on the herd had been going on long enough for Alhia to watch the moon go from a full bright circle to just a sliver. He often varied the time of day he went out in order to observe the animals under different conditions. Which meant he often swam through crowded passageways. Word had gotten around about the experiments he was doing. Most thought he was crazy and avoided him. He liked those people. Unfortunately, a few were curious and pestered him with questions.

He stopped at the entrance to the galley. He didn't want to go in, but it had been a full axial rotation of the planet since he last ate. His stomach was grumbling too much for him to put it off any longer. Kicking out with his feet propelled him across the threshold. His eyes were locked on his destination; the algae dispenser. A few crewmen were in the room, but none reacted to his appearance. He grabbed a resealable container, and filled it with the nutrient-packed green slime. He was in a rush, and the pabulum flowed slowly from the tap. Then a clump fell into the jar and the rest filled up quickly. He turned the spigot off and secured his portion. All he had to do was get to the door. His plan was to eat it on the shuttle. The flights and their guaranteed isolation had become the highlight of his day.

With the exit in sight, he took off. No one in his peripheral vision moved. All he had to do was make it to the corridor and he'd be able to escape to his ship without getting trapped in a conversation. He was almost to the open hatch when suddenly Ophis blocked his way.

"Any milk yet?"

Alhia's body sagged in defeat. "I explained this to you the last time we spoke: The cows have only recently been impregnated. They have to go through their entire gestational period and give birth before their mammary glands will produce milk."

"Well, how long's that going to take?"

"I don't know. I haven't worked with this species before. It will be at least two lunar cycles. But you don't need to keep track. I'm sure there will be a ship-wide announcement if I am successful."

"Yeah, I bet you're right." The young enlisted man started to get out of the way, but then stopped when he thought of something else he wanted to say. "You know, I heard those beasts carry all sorts of parasites around concealed in their fur. Don't you bring any of those back to the ship with you."

The scientist took a deep breath and closed his eyes. When he was sure he could speak without raising the volume, he opened them. "The fleas and mites on the animals all breathe air. They will drown as soon as they are submerged in water. So if I did manage to overlook one that would be clearly visible on my hairless body, there is no way it could infest the ship."

No longer willing to wait for the other man to get out of his way, Alhia swam around him. He had stopped to chat with that crewman, just like he had all the others, because he was being polite. All that it had gotten him was delays in his schedule. None of the comments were insightful or inspiring. Most were just the request for the same information over and over again. The repetition was annoying, but not near as frustrating as the fact that most inquisitors couldn't understand him when he did answer their questions. They had no interest in hearing the details of his work. They all just wanted to know when they were going to get a glass of milk.

In the cockpit, after he ate, he felt better. He wasn't sure how much of his annoyance was because of what had happened and how much was low glucose levels. While he was willing to concede that hunger probably contributed to his mood, he was not willing to repeat the experience on a full stomach to find out. He had too much to do anyway.

He flew a wide arc around the herd. The first few days after he had delivered the serum, this was as close as he got. He used the time to observe the animals and was thankful to not see any changes in them. All the alterations he had initiated were on a cellular level. If there had been any visible changes, it would have been an indication that something had gone seriously wrong.

The herd was grazing near the river. Their location each day seemed to be completely random. He landed just to the east, no longer having to worry about the engine noise startling them. He spent a few moments just watching them mill about. The first day he touched down next to them without their getting spooked, he just stayed in the pilot's seat, not wanting to risk ruining the moment.

As he lowered the ramp, a couple cows meandered past it. One looked up at him as he walked down, but then she went back to eating. The changes in the animals were striking. Where they had been skittish, they were now calm.

It had been a slow process getting the cattle used to him walking in their midst. He was grateful to see some self-preservation was still present. He didn't want them to let predators walk right up to them. But he was out there at least once each daylight, and they seemed to recognize him.

He stepped into the herd. If he got close enough to touch, the cow would move away in the same plodding they used to move to the next clump of grass. Taking hold of the strap on his shoulder, he eased his pack to the ground. There was a warm, steaming pile of manure next to him. While that was something he normally avoided, he needed to run tests to ensure their health. He scooped up a portion of the waste and then confirmed the container was tightly sealed before putting it back.

After twisting the top off of a second sample kit, he wondered if he'd be able to get the specimen he wanted. That was when a cow, ass towards him, lifted her tail. His instinctual reaction was to move away. Instead, he stuck his arm out as far as it would reach, and stepped towards the stream of urine. He was able to catch enough to fill the jar up halfway, more than enough for the analysis he had in mind. He closed the top and used the other hand to put it back in the bag. The soiled hand stayed stretched away from his torso until he was able to get a few paces away and shake it off. He was not able to get all of the splatter off, but enough so that what remained would dry.

The last thing he took out of the case was a long tube. He needed a DNA sample from one of the bovine. Getting one might be a little tricky. While they were more docile, he didn't think they would be content with him getting a sample that wasn't a waste product they were already excreting.

He walked up to a cow facing away from him, and gently placed a hand on her rump. She stepped forward, like he had given her a sign to move ahead. If he did get to the point of collecting milk, he would have to be a lot more hands on with the animals, but that was not something he wanted to rush. He had time to get them slowly used to being touched. In the meantime, he needed a way to confirm the genetic mutations were there.

Staring at the heifer that had just moved away from him, he wondered how she'd react if he pulled out a tuft of her hair. If he got the roots, it would be a viable source of genetic material, though it would also cause her pain. That might keep him from getting close to that animal, and maybe the others, in the future.

Just when he was about to give up and take a clump of fur, he noticed that she was salivating heavily as she ate. It wasn't the best DNA source, but since it wouldn't cause the animal any discomfort collecting it, it made sense to try.

He put his hand on her back, and just like she had before, she lumbered forward. When her sharp hooves were clear of the area he was interested in, he bent over and scooped up the drool.

With that complete, he had everything he needed. Usually, he'd take a while to wander through the herd, letting them get used to his presence, but that was when he didn't have urine splattered on half of his body. He hiked back to the shuttle and set the pack on the ramp instead of climbing it. He knew swimming alone in the sea was prohibited, but doubted there could be any predators large enough to endanger him in the river. He hated the idea of bring the foul odors into the confined space of the cockpit. It was worth the risk for him to clean off.

From the bank, the water seemed to be calling him with its quiet roar. He walked out until he knees were submerged. It was clear enough that he could see the rocky bottom slope away from him. He sprang up, then came down with a splash in the deeper pool. The current was stronger than anything he was used to. It felt exhilarating to push against it. A few small fish were startled by his appearance. He laughed and continued past them. While the powerful currents offered a thrilling experience, the area was too small to really swim in. Just widening his arc had brought him back into the shallows. He stood up, letting the water run off his skin, reinflated his lungs, and headed back to the ship feeling unsullied.

***

The tests confirmed the new DNA strand in the cattle. Alhia had been confident it had worked, but it was a relief to see the proof. He ran the test a second time, just to make sure it wasn't a fluke. By the time he looked at identical results, he could feel the fatigue from all the work he had done. He fell asleep as soon as he was secure in his hammock.

In the morning, he was too busy for small talk, or anything else. Thankfully he had stocked up with enough food for two days the day before, and it was already in the shuttle waiting for him. He rushed through the passageway, past the couple of crewmates waving him over to chat. He didn't acknowledge them, just swam past at full speed. His hands were empty; no equipment was needed for what he had planned, so nothing slowed him down.

To break up the monotony of the flight, he veered slightly to the north. There were rolling hills and then mountains that had been eroded to rounded peaks. It was there he came to the starting point of the two rivers. He turned south, and watched them grow as more streams and rivers merged into the gushing water.

Then he noticed a group of animals headed south in a single line. This was not the defensive clusters herbivories stayed in. He pulled up their image, and confirmed they were clearly predators, with claws and sharp fangs. They were moving towards the grazing lands where he had last seen his herd.

The individual members of the pack were much smaller than the cows, but there were fifteen adults strung along the trail with a couple younger ones mixed in. If they worked together, which was very possible with the way they traveled, it would be very easy for them to take down much larger prey.

He had already planned on moving the herd that day, but with the pack's speed they would be in position to attack by the time the sun was high in the sky. He didn't want to lose any specimen, nor did he want to risk the herd getting scattered as they fled. The relocation was going to be time-consuming by itself; he did not want the complication of having to search for the animals.

He circled around and hovered high over the pack, pacing them as they ran. It took him a moment to estimate how much each canine weighed, confirm the entire pack was within his lifting capabilities, and then widen the beam to capture all of them. They rose up off the ground, midstride. Most of them kept their legs pumping despite the fact they were no longer making contact with the ground.

He crossed the river, but wasn't confident that would be a sufficient barrier to keep them away. From their speed, he calculated how far they could travel in one day and then flew twice that far. The area looked familiar. Then he recognized the hilltop he had landed on when he needed to calm down. The wide open space without trees was the perfect area to set down his cargo. Even if they were able to know what direction to travel and started as soon as he released them, the herd would still be moved to safety before they arrived. He set down the pack in the long line he had picked them up in. They continued running, now in the opposite direction.

He found the bovines clustered on the bank of the river, taking turns getting a drink. He set the controls to stay in a hover and turned his attention to the scanning equipment. Normally working on a microscopic level, he rarely used most of the features. It took a while of scrolling to find what he was looking for, but eventually got it to display the electrical impulses from cardiac muscle. Then he went from animal to animal looking for the ones that not only had a heart beat in their chest, but also in their uterus. Each time he found one, he hoisted the cow until it was suspended in midair.

After the fourth one, the engine had to increase power to hold up the heavy load. He steered the aircraft south. He dropped down over the cliff, and then rose again to keep from running the cattle into the top of a tree. He longed to once again work with just the basic building blocks of life, but he knew what he was about to achieve was worth the struggle.

He had to focus to set his load down gently, then he stayed nearby to observe their reaction. At first, they seemed unsure and huddled together, but eventually they put their heads down and ate. With a sigh of relief, he turned the shuttle around and climbed back up over the sheer rock face.

Upon his return, the herd seemed the same as when he had flown in earlier. The loss of four cows wasn't apparent from the air. This trip went a little faster, since the equipment was already set up. Down river, he lowered the second quartet down in close proximity to the first, but far enough away he didn't have to worry about one coming down on the other. The two groups quickly blended once they were all safely on the ground.

Returning from his fourth trip, the herd was visibly reduced in numbers, even though he had only taken one fifth of the animals. This trip would be the last. He opened up a fresh bottle of water, took a few bites of algae, and then got into position to hoist the last four cows. By the time he finished, it was dark enough that two planets were visible on the western horizon.

Chapter Seven

"Do you have a glass of milk for us yet?"

Alhia closed his eyes and sighed. They were no longer content with ambushing him in the common spaces; now they were coming to his quarters to do it. Their willingness to cross his personal boundaries shouldn't come as a surprise to him, yet it was. He had hoped to have one place he could call his own.

He opened his eyes, looked up and saw Sauries, the ship's psychologist, standing in the doorway. The two golden bands on her arm were a reminder that she was a commissioned officer. Her light green coloring was a beauty rarely found and she was one of the few females on board whom even his eyes were drawn to, but she never used her appearance to gain favors. She was one of the only people on the administrative staff, other than the captain, he had respect for. He bit back the flippant response he had planned and looked down.

"Um, no."

"I was joking." She swam in, smiling. "I know there would be an announcement if you had. I actually came here to see if you need any help."

Startled, he backed into the shelves. She laughed at him as he caught items he had knocked down. None of the scientists had volunteered to assist him, and it seemed strange that now one of the military crew would—and an officer to boot. The enlisted seemed more likely to be the sort willing to get their hands dirty. She completely took him by surprise.

"Are you sure you really want to do that?"

"Yes, I am." She looked at him with a serious expression and her back straight. "My motives are not altruistic."

She stood with shoulders back, her eyes locked on his. She was serious about wanting to help. Intrigued by what she said, he pushed away from the shelves and faced her with his arms open and face free of any preconceived emotions. He was ready to hear how they could have a symbiotic relationship.

"Our unique situation has forced us all into group dynamics not commonly endured by our race. A lot of my studies were in sociology, since the years in space force us to share quarters. We were all prepared for that. It was interesting to watch the social interactions as cliques were formed and dissidence emerged, but all of that has been documented since space travel began. The unnatural confinement normally ends when we reach the destination.

"That wasn't the case for us. It was just the beginning of our ordeal. Like most of our crew, this experience has challenged my professional abilities. I've had to learn to look for answers in unorthodox locations, so I've been studying the group dynamics of the marine mammals we added to the planet and even the native life forms. I'm curious to see if the interactions of the land creatures are similar to the ones in the ocean."

When she was done speaking, she swam around the room, looking at different machines and supplies he had stored on shelves. He watched her, wondering what someone used to talking to people all day would be able to do to help him. She didn't have a scientific background. She had minimal medical training, none of which would transfer over to terrestrial mammals. But it seemed foolish to say no to the one person that had offered to assist him. Who knew?, Maybe with her military training, she might be able to offer a perspective completely different that his.

"I'm worried that any information you're looking for would be compromised by the gene alterations I've done." He cocked his head to one side.

She was on the far side of the room staring at a diagram of a gene, and she turned around to look at him. Her head cocked to the side as she thought about what he said. After a moment, her head leveled and she said, “Really? I thought your work changed the interactions the animals had with other species, but not within members of the herd.”

It was his turn to pause and reflect. “Through the course of my experiments, I have observed their behaviors before and after the virions were delivered. I admit, while their behavior towards me has changed dramatically, I have seen very little change with how they interact with each other. You may, after all, gather insight by observing them.” He made eye contact with her, which was usually uncomfortable with other people, but she smiled in response.

“When in large groups, instinctual behavior can become more prominent. So studying lesser intelligent animals can help me understand what’s going on with us.” She now swam around in circles, buoyed by their conversation.

“You are not joking about the less intelligent part.” His eyes widened as he spoke.

She stopped circling and graced him with a beautiful smile. Her serious demeanor faded away, leaving her relaxed and happy. “When are you headed out again?”

“I was just getting ready to leave. Would you like to join me?”

Her eyes lit up, and she danced about. He rolled his eyes, grabbed his tote, led the way through the open hatch, and up through the spiraling corridor. She quickly caught up to him, and stayed right beside him the whole way. The crewman they passed all stared, probably assuming he was doing something for the command. He was grateful no one tried to flag him down to talk to him.

She didn't say anything at the transition pool; which was another thing he was thankful for. They both went right into their own routines. He noticed that her order of doing things seemed very haphazard, but refrained from commenting since he would have to ruin the silence to do so. They actually made it all the way into the shuttle without saying a word.

"Where should I sit?" Sauries asked.

"Wherever you want."

Alhia motioned to the empty rows in the passenger compartment. Neither his arm nor his gaze extended to the front cabin. She took that as an indication she wasn't supposed to sit up there. She felt like she was in his way, so she lowered herself into a seat in the front row while he stowed the gear.

In the pilot's seat, Alhia finished the preflight check list and started the engines. It was late enough for the sun to have risen above eye level, so he was able to program a direct route. Once he reached altitude and the course was set, he pulled up the record for the weather for the last few days and had the system calculate the most likely weather for the immediate future. He had noticed some variations in predominate currents for the specific area and factored in those. He was still lost in the data when the alarm indicated he was starting to descend.

As usual, he checked the herd from the air before landing. He picked a landing site close the animals, and as level as he could find. Sauries stood up as he made his way through the craft. She was quiet and stayed out of the way; he liked that. He stopped at the back storage compartment and pulled out the top tote with the basic supplies. He reached into the cabinet and grabbed the handle of the sample kit. Then he relaxed his fingers and withdrew his empty hand. His companion had stepped into his peripheral vision, reminding him he would be too busy being a tour guide and looking after her to get much work done.

Sauries lowered the ramp and stared out at the world being revealed to her. He waited for a reaction that never happened. Her eyes just skimmed over the animals in her line of sight. When the ramp locked into place, she climbed down it. He was right behind her, descending to the hard-packed dirt.

He expected her to stop once her feet touched soil. All she wanted to do was observe the mammals, and she could do that from where she stood. To his surprise, she kept walking across the grassland. She kept her eyes on the cattle instead of on the ground in front of her. Her toe caught in a divot, and she stumbled to her knees.

"I should have warned you." He helped her up. "The ground here can be very uneven and rocky. It's best to assess where you're about to step, before you put your foot down."

She did as he said, making sure the path was clear before each step. The difficulty was she didn't want to stop looking at the creatures. So, she would look down, move one foot forward, and then look back up to see if any of the animals had done anything. It made her progress very slow. The one time she tried to skip looking down, she lost her balance and almost went down again. Alhia was there, at her elbow, steadying her.

"Oh, I don't mean to keep you from your work. You should go on ahead." She held her head down.

"Do you want to go back to the shuttle?" He turned around like he was ready to take her back.

"Oh, no." She pulled on his hand until he had swung back around to face the cattle. "I'm just fine on my own."

She didn't seem alright by herself. She had almost fallen down twice and would have the second time if he hadn't been there to catch her, but her eyes held his with a determination he didn't see very often.

"Are you sure? I've had more practice walking on dry ground."

"Which means I am holding you up. This is not my first time out of the water. I will be fine. I just need a few minutes for my muscles to remember how to balance."

He looked at her for a moment before doing what she asked. He was all ears as he stepped away from her, waiting to her hear her cry out in pain from stumbling again. The only wail he heard was one of the cows on the far side of the herd. He looked in that direction but didn't see any reason for the sudden outburst. He shook his head and kept walking.

About halfway to the first cow, he stopped and looked back at her. Her eyes were focused on the ground as she walked past a cluster of rocks. When she looked up and saw him watching her, she smiled. She was obviously doing fine on her own, even if she was going slow. Maybe he would get some work done. He took pictures of the cow's udders, with scale markings, to document the changes. He could tell many of them were starting to enlarge. The animals didn't shift as he walked near them. They didn't even seem to notice him.

A heifer bellowed, and then he heard Sauries' laugh come from the same direction. He looked over, but didn't see her. He took a step in the direction the noises had come from when her head popped up between two cows. She was grinning ear to ear as she ran her hand over the animal's midsection.

He was blown away. He hadn't thought anyone would come out with him, let alone touch the beasts. The idea of touching fur repulsed most of his kind. He was used to people staying in their stereotypical roles, so Sauries had shocked him in more ways than one.

"You know they're going to go into labor soon," she said when she noticed him looking at her.

"I haven't been able to get an exact length of gestation, but I figure the calves will start coming before the new moon."

She stopped petting the animal and walked over to him with her head tilted to the side. "Can I come back with you when you collect the milk?"

"Well, I guess so." His eyes were large. "I have to warn you, it's bound to be messy. All of our collection systems are designed to be used on marine life. I don't know how well it will adapt. I'm probably going to have to do it by hand."

She smirked. "As you can see, I'm not afraid to get close to them."

Chapter Eight

After Sauries insisted that she join Alhia, she stood next to him staring at the afterbirth. The no-longer-needed organ that had transferred nutrients from the mother to the fetus lay on the ground next to the newborn calf. Both were covered in slime.

"It looks like cheese," she said between bouts of nausea. "I've been looking forward to getting it, and suddenly I don't want it anymore."

"Maybe it tastes like cheese?" He shrugged. "The cow has no aversion to licking it off the newborn, so it can't taste that bad."

She gave him a derisive look. "I don't think it has anything to do with taste."

The mother finished cleaning off her baby, then ate the placenta. Even Alhia had to turn away from that. Sauries managed to get two steps before stomach cramps drove her to her knees. With quick, short breaths, she managed to keep from regurgitating.

"I thought you said they were herbivores?" She turned to glare at him.

"I did." He gave her a bewildered look. "I've only seen them eat grass."

"Then why would they do…" She waived at the scene behind her. "That?"

He thought about it for a moment. "I think it might be a survival technique. The mess would draw in scavengers and possibly predators. By getting rid of it themselves, they don't have to worry about what else will be lured here by the scent."

"I guess that makes sense. Neither of them appeared able to flee for their lives at the moment." She shivered with another wave of nausea, even though she was looking away from the gore. "Knowing the reason doesn't make it any less gross."

"No, it doesn't." He helped her to her feet and away from the scene. "Let's give them space to do what they must. I'm very excited to see how swollen the udders are. Last year their mammary parenchyma was much smaller. I still need to see how much the calf consumes before we attempt to collect any milk. We must first ensure the survival of the herd before we can see if there is any surplus."

Walking helped. Her abdomen relaxed and stopped feeling like it was going to revolt. The whole experience left her weak. She sat down on the ramp and finally felt a little better. The scene wasn't so grisly from afar.

Alhia felt relieved when her symptoms subsided. He thought he was going to have to take her back to the Catenata, but slowly the color returned to her cheeks and her shoulders pulled back until her spine was in its normal upright position. As her appearance improved, she started talking. Nothing of consequence, just little tidbits about her home world and the one other mission she had been on. He normally wasn't one for small talk, but was surprised at how easy she made it.

"Look, the calf is already trying to walk." She sat upright and pointed.

He looked where they had just been standing, and the fuzzy little baby was attempting to stand on wobbly legs. He fell time and time again, but he kept trying. Eventually he figured out how to stay upright and then took three unsteady steps over to his mother. He went directly to her udder and started nursing. It seemed hunger was a powerful motivator for this species. He thought that was strange, since he would often forget to eat.

Alhia and Sauries wandered back into the herd. All the mess of the afterbirth had been cleaned up. They didn't want to disturb the animals, so both ended up standing there awkwardly, just watching the calf eat. The young cow suckled from the teat longer than they had anticipated. Sauries was the first to get bored and wander away. He looked over his shoulder and watched her meander farther into the herd.

There was another cow that looked like it would be giving birth in the next couple days. He palpated the abdomen, and could easily ascertain the fetus' limbs. He estimated it to be the same size as the one now eating. From there, he walked closer to the river to so the same assessment on another heifer. When that one was done, he looked around, trying to guess which cow would go into labor next. But before he could come up with an idea, a scream rang out.

Alhia spun around to see Sauries running across the field. The cow behind her no longer looked docile, it was now snorting and its sharp hooves dug into the sod as it chased her. The bovine gained ground on her, even though Sauries ran at full speed.

With no time to think, he ran towards them. He had no idea what he was going to do. He didn't have anything to defend himself with, not even a rock to throw. The beast bearing down on them was five times their size and seemed fixated on her destruction. That was something he couldn't let happen. His only hope was to outsmart the animal, and he prayed he had time to do that.

Sauries slipped on the grass and went down with the creature still barreling towards her. Alhia was just steps away and took a stance with a foot planted on either side of her. He raised his arms up, hoping to look larger than he actually was. The animal let out a loud sound, with saliva hanging from both sides of its mouth. Not knowing that else to do, he bellowed back just as loudly.

Bracing for impact, the scientist was sure the crew would find their dead bodies in that exact spot. At the last second, the cow changed course and ran past them. He twisted around to keep the beast in sight, sure that as soon as he wasn't looking it would attack. The animal circled around them. He felt trapped, knowing they were too slow to get away if they did decide to run. All he could do was stand his ground, while Sauries got to her feet next to him. He gave her a quick glance, not wanting to look away from the threat. She looked unharmed. Their breathing was hard and labored but eventually slowed.

The cow continued running laps around them, but eventually went into a trot. Her anger seemed to have dissipated. Then her calf called out, drawing her attention away from the pair standing in the middle of the field. At first, she seemed torn, not knowing what to do. But eventually she went back to her infant and let it suckle, keeping an eye on them the whole time.

Sauries gripped Alhia's arm tightly, so when he took a step back, she went with him. They walked backwards to keep an eye on the potential danger, but the cow never budged. Once they were clear of the herd, they turned around and walked normally to the aircraft. Neither of them bothered to board it, opting to sit on the ramp instead.

"I'm so sorry." He hung his head down. "I had assumed the gene alterations had tamed them. I should have done more testing to confirm that before I brought you out here. I will have to go back and report that I am a failure."

"I'm not sure that you are." She met his gaze when he turned to her in disbelief. "I've wandered through the herd many times touching just about every animal. There has never been a problem until I touched the newborn, and then it was only the mother that became upset."

"They're protective of their young?" His eyebrows raised.

"Yes." There was excitement in her eyes. "This reaction might help explain why life had filled every niche on this planet. In the ocean, very few lifeforms do anything more than lay eggs and leave. Though I have seen a couple species that help the young reach maturity. I would really like to study more land animals and see if this is common here."

"I hope you find a way to test your theory that doesn't involve putting yourself in harm's way," he said seriously.

"Definitely." She looked at him and smiled. "If you hadn't been there, I would have been stomped into the dirt. Thank you."

He tentatively smiled back, then turned his attention to the animals wandering in front of them. They both sat there in silence, watching the cattle graze. The scene looked just like it always did. There wasn't any sign of the excitement that had just happened.

"Look over there at that cow." She pointed at one on the edge of the herd. "It has milk dripping from its teats, but I don't see a calf with it."

"Really? Where?" He looked to where she gestured. "I saw the remains of a dead calf when we flew in. I wonder if it was hers."

"And you didn't bring it to my attention?" Her hands were on her hips.

"I thought this planet had exposed you to enough death. I did not think you needed to see anymore." His brows pulled in as he spoke. Before she could respond, he added "Can I get your help?"

"Of course." She straightened her back. "What do you have in mind?"

She was left sitting there without an answer. He got up and went into the shuttle. When he came out, his hands were full. She took part of the load, and followed him into the herd. He went straight to the cow she had pointed out.

"Can you distract the animal for me?"

"What do you mean?" She gave him a skeptical look.

"I don't know. Just do something to keep the cow's attention off of me."

Sauries nodded, even though she was not really sure what was expected of her. What would entertain a furry land mammal? She had no idea. All they seemed to do was eat. She picked some grass and held it up to the cow's mouth. It sniffed at her offering, but didn't take any. She dropped the plant matter and ran her hands over the animal's long face.

"I don't think this one is feeling very well."

"What makes you say that?"

"Her eyes aren't as focused as the other animal's. Her reaction time also seems to be slower." She leaned around the cow as she spoke. "Do you think she's mourning the loss of her baby?"

Alhia looked over from where he squatted next to the cow. "I would have said no this morning, but now I wonder."

The animal liked to have its head scratched between its ears; looking up at her for the first time when she did. Sauries was happy to get positive results from what she was doing, and continued rubbing the fur in that area. At first the cow was content, but then kept trying to look around.

"I don't think it's very happy with you being back there."

"Well, it's not snorting and trying to trample us, so it's not too upset." There was a pause and then he said, "Wow. I got it."

Warm milk streamed down into the container on the ground. Each squeeze of his hand produced another squirt.

"She calmed down. I think she likes that." She continued petting.

"Her udders were distended. I imagine this is giving her relief."

The ewer was almost filled by the time he was done with all four teats. The smell of the white frothy liquid had him salivating. It even had him longing for home; a reaction he hadn't anticipated. By the time he was done, his lower extremities had cramped up. He placed his hands on the side of the cow to steady himself as he stood. The cow stepped forward, kicking the milk. He lunged forward, caught the jar as it tipped over and sprawled out on the ground underneath the animal. The sudden movement startled the cow, and it stepped on him to get away from the commotion.

Sauries had jumped back to get clear of the animal. "What happened? Was there any milk?"

"There was." He winced in pain, but managed to roll over to show her the wet spot on the ground. He looked in the jug. "Well, there is a little bit left."

He handed her the pitcher. Her limbs trembled and she had rapid and shallow breaths. He hadn't seen anyone that excited, not anyone that had reached full maturity, anyway. She had the container up to her mouth, but stopped before tipping it up.

"There is not much here. You've done all the work. You should have it."

He shook his head. "You have done a lot, too. Besides, I was hoping if I let you drink it, you wouldn't tell anyone I spilt it."

"That will be our secret." She tipped up the jar.

"Well, how was it?" He leaned his head toward her as he asked.

"Wonderful." She licked her lips. "I don't know how it would compare to our home world, but after going without it, it is phenomenal."

"Tonight, I will try to come up with a better collection system." His demeanor was once again serious. "I would recommend not saying anything to the rest of the crew. There is a chance the milk could dry up overnight. I wouldn't want everyone to resent you because you got the only sip."

Chapter Nine

Sauries followed Alhia into the shuttle at dawn the next day. This time, she didn't take her normal seat in the passenger compartment. Instead, she followed him into the cockpit and sat down in the copilot seat. He froze as she settled in but didn't say anything or change his facial expression. After a moment, he got into the seat next to her and started the preflight checklist like nothing had happened.

To his relief, there weren't any more gruesome scenes on the way in. The way she stayed pressed against the windows the entire flight, she would have been the one to point it out if there had been. She looked out the glass until they were coming in to land. To his relief, she didn't comment about anything she saw in passing. In fact, she didn't say anything until the ramp was lowered.

"Look, there is another calf."

He looked over where she indicated, and there was another newborn very close to the one that had been born the day before. He had no idea how long it was going to be between births and was glad to see them coming one after another.

"It must have been born during the night."

They both stopped at the bottom of the ramp and looked over the herd. Then looked to see if the evidence of the birth had been cleaned up before proceeding any farther. When they didn't see any trace of the placenta, they closed the gap between them and the closest animal.

The two calves stayed close to their mothers. Both gave the babies and their dams plenty of space, not wanting to cause another incident. After a little bit of circling through the heifers, they finally found the one that had lost her calf. She looked better than she had the day before. To his surprise, her udder was full and ready to be milked again. He was grateful she hadn't dried up like the aquatic mammals did. Alhia could not be certain that it was because of gene alteration; maybe life if the ocean was more arduous. Either way, he was collecting the rewards.

He had stayed up late and gone to the galley after everyone else had gone to bed. There he had found non-permeable sacks that he could use to collect the milk. The top sealed, so he could close it as soon as it was full. The flexible material would be easier to use in the field than the rigid container he had used the day before—or at least he hoped it would.

Before he had a chance to ask, Sauries was at the head, scratching the cow between the ears. He wouldn't have thought of that, but it seemed to be an adequate distraction. He knelt down beside the udder and slipped one of the bags over a teat. He was able to squeeze the milk directly into the bag. After he had finished all four, the bag was almost filled. He folded the top over and closed the seal. He set the bag on the ground and pushed himself up. Sauries saw that he was finished and patted the cow on the head.

"Good job. You feel better now, don't you?"

She stepped out of the animal's way so it could go back to grazing. The cow took the cue and stepped forward. Alhia had his back arched and was looking straight up at the sky to stretch the tight muscles in his neck. The smell of milk hit his nostrils. At first he closed his eyes. Maybe he had spent enough time procuring the stuff that the odor of it was trapped in his nasal passages. But then, as the odor got stronger, he realized that couldn't be the cause. He looked down, to see the cow's hoof had sliced open the bag, and the precious liquid was pouring out onto the ground. He quickly bent over, picked it up, and held it so that the open section was at the top.

"Again?" Sauries asked.

He sighed, not wanting to respond. He finally made eye contact and shrugged. "This is why I didn't let anyone know that I was collecting milk today. When dealing with wild creatures, you never know what can go wrong." He looked back down at the fluid in his hand. "At least there is enough for both of us, this time."

He didn't even offer; he just took the first drink. It was warmer than he expected and coated his mouth and throat as he swallowed. The taste reminded him of home and all the great things he had been without on this mission. He had only meant to take a sip, but he had ended up gulping down half the container. He held the milk out to her, before he could change his mind and finish it.

She took the bag, but didn't immediately drink from it. First, she looked at him questioningly, and only put it to her lips when he nodded for her to go ahead. Unlike him, she slowly quaffed. When she was done, she took a deep breath and handed the container back to him. The sack was damaged beyond repair, so it was crumpled and put in the bottom of the tote with the other things that needed to be disposed of.

With bellies full of the something they had been denied for so long, they had renewed motivation to collect more. They both turned and looked at the two new mothers. The calves were playing together between them, with no interest in eating at the moment. Both udders still looked engorged. The calves looked similar enough that they could not identify which had been born first.

"Well, it's time to see if I've been successful." He pulled his shoulders back. "Their udders still look full, but there's only one way to make sure."

"I think positioning is going to be important," Sauries cautioned. "They seem perturbed when their calf isn't in sight."

He nodded in agreement with what she said, but he didn't step forward. Instead, he eyed the animals warily.

"They're so calm right now, but I remember what this animal turns into when they're not happy."

"So don't touch the babies." She stepped up and petted the closest mother between her ears. The cow leaned into the touch. "That's the only thing we've found that triggers a bad reaction."

"So far."

With her leading the way, he felt silly being cautious. He picked up the tote and carried it to the animal's side. He set a hand on the cow's rump before he set the case down. Only when he didn't get a rise from her did he go ahead and assemble the gear he needed.

Sauries stayed at the cow's head, making sure to not get directly between the mom and the baby. This wasn't as easy as she had thought it would be; the little ones were very energetic and bounced all over the place. Thankfully, momma cow seemed just as worn out from watching them as she was.

Both new mothers took to milking the same way the other cow had. He collected half a bag from each of them. He had learned from his previous mistakes, so no more was spilled. Still, it didn't seem like much when he was done.

"Don't worry about it," she said when she saw him frown. "This is just the beginning."

"How can you be so sure?" His expression didn't change.

"Because there are about sixteen more cows getting ready to give birth. When we collect milk from all of them, it's going to add up. Before you know it, we'll have a cooler filled with aging cheese and enough for the crew to drink."

He stretched his strained extremities, suddenly understanding why no one wanted to work on land. You didn't have to crouch down under aquatic mammals, and the constant swimming to stay beside them kept muscles from cramping up. The walk back to the shuttle loosened him up. He went about securing his tools while she stood by the seats.

"What do you think we should do with it?" she asked.

"I considered taking back to the lab and sharing it with the other scientist, since there isn't enough for everyone."

"That's one idea. I'm just worried they will talk and you'll end up creating discord."

"You know what? You're right. This decision should be left to someone used to being in charge."

***

The docking clamps clicked as they locked in place. Alhia looked to his right, and Sauries smiled at him. He managed to stop frowning for a moment, feeling his mouth form a straight line in response.

"You've done what none of the biologists on this crew were able to do. You've given us milk."

He huffed. "Not enough. If we divided it equally amongst all the crew members, it wouldn't be enough for them to even taste it."

"Today, it isn't enough," she countered with a quick raise of her eyebrows. "But these animals aren't like the whales. They are producing more and don't show any signs of drying up. I have faith that this is just the beginning."

"Well, I'm not a man to believe in anything until I see the results."

With that said, he got up and went to the back of the cabin. Technically, he could have left the tote right where it was. He didn't need anything out of it until he went back out in the field. But he needed something to carry the milk in. He could just carry the bag, but then if they passed anyone in the corridor they would be able to see what he had. Not wanting word to get out, he pulled the tote out of the storage compartment, then put the white liquid inside.

As he expected, there wasn't anyone between the shuttle and the transition pool. The only ones he ever ran into above the water line were engineers going in or out of the engine compartment, and that was rare. But to his surprise, he made it down to the officer's staterooms without seeing anyone else. That might be because he stopped at the first door before the galley. As he pressed the button to announce his arrival, Sauries waited next to him. He had expected her to go on to her own quarters, but he certainly wasn't going to discourage her from being a part of this after all the help she had provided.

"Enter," Yosheia called out.

They went through the hatch and found themselves in an empty room. There were things along each wall to serve guests, but no work space or place to sleep. There was another door to their left. That was where they found the Captain reading over logs on the monitor. While they both patiently waited for him to finish, Alhia looked through the next doorway and saw a sleeping hammock.

Tired eyes finally looked up from the memorandum. The old man sighed, looking like he didn't want to deal with anything else. The scientist realized he had never seen the commanding officer after hours or in private. He had only observed the C.O. in public settings, where the man looked chipper and ready to take on anything. He wondered if this drastic change in appearance was a daily thing, or new from the strain of the mission. The geneticist couldn't think of anything to say that seemed right, at least not anything that didn't sound trite. So instead of speaking, he opened up the tote and withdrew the bag inside.

Yosheia's eyes grew large when he saw the milk. He blinked a few times, like he didn't believe what he was seeing. He leaned forward, as if he had forgotten how to stay upright. Then he kicked out with his feet and glided across the room.

"Is that…?"

Silence hung in the air as the two guests waited for him to finish the question. Alhia and Sauries looked at each other and shrugged. When they looked back at the senior officer, his expression was of someone waiting for an answer. He seemed unaware he never completed his inquiry.

Realizing they were never going to hear the end of the sentence, the scientist nodded and said, “Yes.”

Yosheia trembled, then swam circles around the other two. Sauries laughed at the jubilant display. The C.O. finally came to a stop in front of them with his upper extremities still shaking.

“May I?”

Apparently they weren’t going to get more than 2 words at a time out of the man.

“Yes, you may.” Alhia handed over the pouch.

Yosheia held out both hands, slowly reaching out for the precious gift. He noticed that his hands quivered and pulled them back. With his eyes on the on the deck, he swallowed large gulps of water and focused on the feeling of it streaming across his gills. After ten gulps, he felt calmer. When he looked at his hands, they were finally steady, so he extended his arms back out, his fingers cupped.

For a few moments, the captain just stared at the white fluid, almost as if it would disappear if he took his eyes off it. Eventually his gaze did return to the bearer of his gift. Their eyes stayed locked until the geneticist gave him another nod.

The C.O. tore the first tab off the seal, and pressed the bag to his lips. The first sip was small. As soon as the frothy liquid hit his taste buds, all the tension in his body melted. He lifted the bag higher and started gulping down the milk like he had the water, only this was going down his esophagus and into his digestive tract.

By the time he stopped, half the contents were gone. The only reason he stopped was to get water over his gills before he became light-headed. While he got his oxygen levels back up, he asked "Where's the rest of it?"

"That's all."

"For now." Sauries added.

The captain's expression quickly went from disappointment to confusion. His creased brow turned to the lieutenant. "I wasn't aware you were helping with this project."

She assumed the position of attention. "Yes, sir. I thought the experience would help me study social behaviors. I promise it will not interfere with any of my duties."

"You volunteered?" The captain's eyebrows went up.

"Yes, sir. I did." Her rigid posture relaxed slightly. "I didn't want to pass up any opportunity to learn about group dynamics. For our species it's uncommon, but for these creatures it's natural. I have a chance to see how they live side by side, day in and day out."

"But we don't have any common words with these primitive beasts, do we?"

"No." She laughed. "Their behavior is very instinctual, but the strain of the mission has caused many of us to revert to more basic behaviors."

"Very well, then. Carry on." He turned his attention back to the other man. "When can I expect more of this?"

The scientist suddenly looked very uncomfortable. "I have no way to predict the exact quantities."

Sauries had stayed slightly behind the civilian, but now she moved up next to him. He stopped talking and looked at her.

"I believe we will be able to double the quantities next time we go out. As soon as the remaining calves are born, it will be quadrupled, at least. For the time being, we will not have enough to ration to the crew. We will have to stockpile a few days' supply before everyone can have a sample. That should be easy enough to do with the cold storage in the galley."

He looked guilty for guzzling down half the bag, "So this is not a one-time thing?"

"From all indications, the production should be sustainable," the geneticist reported. "But as of yet I'm unable to predict what the daily output will be or when lactation will cease. I don't want to get everyone's hopes up." Alhia frowned at her.

She didn't let his look of disapproval get to her; in fact, she grinned. "I know you're being conservative for a reason. I'm just reporting what I saw."

The CO gave a curt nod. They both knew this was an indication he had heard enough and had made up his mind. "Well, there's no sense in everyone getting excited about this tonight. I have a small cold storage box I can keep this in. Tomorrow morning I'll talk to Halis about what we need and tell her to keep a lid on this until we can share it with everyone. By the time you get back from…" He paused, struggling to find the right word. "Milking, she'll be ready for you. For the time being, keep bringing it in concealed."

"Yes, sir."

"Thank you." The captain held direct eye contact with Alhia. "This is the best thing that's happened on this mission."

Alhia was surprised that such a simple thing would make such an extreme change, but the proof was right in front of him. Yosheia went from looking overworked to seeming ready to face their remaining time left on the planet. He didn't expect anyone to be this excited, but it appeared having a fresh protein source was going to change everything.

Chapter Ten

For the fourth day in a row, Alhia went straight to the galley after docking the shuttle. Sauries had seen how much he struggled with the task, and accompanied him into the room. As expected, there were a couple crewmen waiting inside with questions. The junior officer fended off the inquiries while he went to the back corner where Halis waited. He was surprised to see the captain at her side.

"Is that it?" The culinary specialist held out her hands towards the tote.

Alhia was taken aback. It had been their habit to both go into the cooler, where he would hand her the milk in private. He was pretty sure everyone on the crew knew what they were doing, even if they didn't actually see the transfer. The C.O.'s head tipped to the side, as if he, too, were waiting for a response. The scientist, still not wanting to expose his cache to the busybodies behind him, slid the strap from his shoulder and handed the carryall over to the petty officer. As soon as it was in her hand, she slipped behind the closed door.

"You must be very excited." Yosheia clapped the civilian on the back.

"Actually, I'm really tired. There are now five cows to milk, and that's a lot of time hunched down. I was going to head to my room."

"In a moment." The senior officer turned. "Lieutenant, can you join us?"

A pipe went out for all hands to muster in the galley. Immediately, people started filing in. A knot formed in the geneticist's stomach, and he backed up until his feet hit the bulkhead. Then Sauries was there at his side. She didn't say anything, but occasionally one of her extremities would bump up against him as they swam in place. Each time it happened, he would glance over at her, but she would be facing the other direction.

He turned back to watch the progress as everyone reported in. There had been a couple all-hands at the beginning of the mission and an advancement ceremony for one of the enlisted. For each of those, Alhia had been on the other side of the room, in the tightly-packed throng of people. But when Kolpos, the executive officer, informed his superior that everyone was there or accounted for, the room was only half full. It was a stark reminder of how devastating this planet had been on the crew.

"Now, getting to the point of why we are all gathered here. This is a monumental day for us. After so many setbacks and all the hardships we've endured, I'm happy to announce we finally have something to celebrate."

The doldrums of the assembled died away as a wave of excitement washed over them. With everyone suddenly shifting around, microcurrents swirled through the vast space. Air bubbles carried by the water added to the festive mood.

"For the first time since we've arrived on this dismal planet," Yosheia continued. "We have fresh milk available to us…"

The roar of the assembled made it impossible to hear what else the CO said. Alhia had never seen a commotion of this magnitude. In shock, he froze in place, even though what he really wanted to do was escape.

"Calm down. Calm down." The captain had to yell to be heard over the furor. It took some time to get order restored, but eventually he did it. "Today we only have enough for each of us to have a sample, but rest assured this is only the beginning. In the weeks to come, we will not only have enough to drink but to also make cheese."

The volume rose again. This time Yosheia didn't try to yell over them. Eventually, the noise level died down enough to hear individual voices.

"Alhia saved the mission," Ferox bellowed.

The geneticist tried to back further away from the crowd, only to have his back hit the wall. He looked to his left. There was no way out. Sauries was on his right, smiling at him. He turned back to the commanding officer, expecting him to say more. Instead, Yosheia faced him, and motioned him to come forward. He shook his head, but the psychologist took his arm and pulled him forward.

Everyone had the wrong idea. He didn't want to be there and really didn't want to talk, but someone had to clear up the misunderstanding.

"This only affects one small part of our mission…" he stopped mid-sentence, unable to hear himself over the racket. Only when the noise level dropped did he try again. "The mutations I pioneered have only been tried on one species. The quantities we will achieve are still unknown, and this is a minor part of our mission. We still face many threats rendering this planet forever unfavorable. My only goal was to make our remaining time here a little easier to bear."

The door behind him opened, and Halis emerged with a stack of white cubes. The six white chevrons on her upper arm stood out as she headed straight into the mob. In no time, her basket was empty and the people at the far edges of the group were handed their serving. All etiquette was ignored as they bit through the capsule and sucked the milk directly from it.

Alhia assumed the excitement would be short-lived, since it only took moments to disperse everything they had stockpiled. Then Halis went around the room, refilling her basket as she collected all the empty containers. There was no further attempt to pretend this was an official meeting. Yosheia disappeared into the masses, happy to take credit for his part in getting the milk. Sauries was pulled off in the other direction, leaving the geneticist by himself in the corner.

No matter which way Alhia looked, there was a wall at least three bodies thick blocking his way out. The formation was no longer keeping an arm's length distance from the person next to them. All of them were pushing in towards him. He turned back to the left, to see if anything had opened up that way, and found Miliaris swimming up to him.

"Isn't this fantastic?" Her arms moved around as she spoke. "When you first suggested this, I had serious doubts about you working with the beasts, but you did it. You really did it."

Movement to Alhia's right made him look that way. Gomesi, the ship's corpsman, approached. "I was beginning to think I'd never taste that again. Thank you so much."

"Really, it was nothing. No thanks required."

"'It was nothing'?" The young petty officer with five white chevrons reached out and took ahold of the scientist's shoulder. "You genetically altered animals. That's not nothing."

"It wasn't a big deal for me." Alhia explained.

"It might not be a big deal for you, but it's a huge deal to us." The microbiologist was back in the conversation. "You need to allow us to express our gratitude to you."

She clung to his left hand. He had to use his right one to get the other one free. Then he spun around to get loose from the grip on his shoulder. "Yep. Got it. You're welcome."

He swam backwards, away from the other two. Not paying attention to where he was going, he ended up surrounded by four others who all wanted to tell him what a great thing he had done. And touch him. Shoulders. Hands. Elbows. Even his face was caressed. Through it all, he kept moving closer and closer to the door. He reminded himself that this is what he wanted for everyone; a little reward for everything they had faced. Eventually, he did manage to slip away and was smiling as he did so.

Chapter Eleven

As Alhia approached the transition pool, he saw four pairs of feet hanging down in the water. He stopped where he was, not wanting to go any further until he knew what was going on. Just the idea of that many people in a normally-unused part of the ship made him nervous. The only explanation he could think of was that there must be a meeting for the military personnel on the bridge. Feeling better that there had to be a simple explanation, one that didn't include him having to interact with people, he propelled himself to the water's surface.

Unable to do his normal move of flying out of the water and twisting into a seated position, he pushed himself up on the ledge and quietly settled amongst the crowd. He quickly glanced around the circle. All of the faces were looking at him.

"Alhia, you're here."

Being addressed was confusing enough. He had spent ninety-five revolutions around this star in forced close proximity to all these people without them speaking to him once. He was very comfortable with things staying that way. The part that confused him was that none of the people sitting at the edge of the pool had opened their mouth. With a feeling of dread, he looked over their heads into the hallway behind them.

It looked like half the crew was milling about in the passageway; some leaned against the wall, some paced back and forth and one sat on the floor. In a panic, the scientist struggled to breath. He looked down at the water's surface, and thought about diving back in to escape. Then he remembered he was sitting in air and wasn't breathing. He sealed his gills and expanded his lungs with a deep breath. When his oxygen levels returned to normal, he was able to be rational once again. No matter what was going on here, he had to tend the herd. So if he focused on completing his routine, he could get into his shuttle and take off.

Tuning out the murmur of voices around him, the geneticist focused on stretching. He began with his neck, moving his head side to side and front and back. With his eyes closed, he could pretend he was alone. After the neck, he moved down to his shoulders; small circles in one direction and then in the other.

"When are we leaving?"

The voice was loud enough to interrupt him. He opened his eyes, expecting to see the others talking back and forth. He was surprised to find everyone looking at him. He looked from face to face, and they all had the same expression, like they were waiting for him to say something.

"Did you ask something?"

"Yeah, when are we leaving?" Tarpon stepped forward out of the hall.

"We?" Alhia's eyes jumped for person to person as they all nodded in response. "All of you?"

Even the people in the far corridor answered yes.

"Why?"

The compartment erupted with noise as everyone responded at the same time. He could pick out a few individual voices, and they all seemed to be saying the same thing: they wanted to come out and see him get the milk. It was like a little extra protein in their diet and made everyone insane.

"Well, you can't all fit into the shuttle, so some of you will have to stay behind."

Kolpos stepped forward. "I am a pilot. I can follow you in a second shuttle."

"No." The scientist jumped up, forgetting about the rest of his stretching routine. "In order to milk the heifers, I must hunch down beside them, in very close proximity to their sharp hooves. I will not have another craft flying around, potentially startling the animals while I'm in a precarious position. There is no sense in any of you going out there, and if you all insist on going today, you can milk the cows yourself."

Kolpos' back went stiff, making him look down on the civilian. "None of us know how to do that."

Alhia stared down the other man. "Then I suggest you figure out which half of you are not going."

The volume spiked as everyone insisted on being in the first group out. Alhia ignored them all, bent over and rubbed his legs. It was an old trick he had learned if you needed to rush through the transition. When that was done, he made his way through the crowd to the entrance to the shuttle. The way was blocked by two enlisted crewman that refused to budge until everything was worked out. They were very aptly concerned he would take off alone.

The passageway went dark. Everyone was silent, not know what had happened. When the lights came back on, Sauries walked into the middle of the group.

"All right, everybody. I know this is exciting, and you all want to be a part of it. We have ten seats available, and I have a quick and fair way to decide who will be on today's flight and who will be joining us tomorrow."

The psychologist made a full circle as she spoke, flashing Alhia a big grin when she got back to him. He was saved. He knew she would take care of the people problem, and all he had to worry about was doing his job with an audience. The two guarding the door were swept away with the others, so he went ahead to check on the supplies.

Once everything was secured, he closed the door on the storage area. Everyone was getting situated, and he wound his way through the people to get to the cockpit. Kolpos was seated in the copilot seat. He turned around and found the usual occupant of the seat at the back of the passenger cabin.

"I need Sauries in the flight cabin with me."

"I don't see how that could be the case," the executive officer replied. "I'm a trained pilot. I can help you fly."

"I don't need a co-pilot. I need my assistant to help me make observations."

"I have eyes. Tell me what to watch for."

Alhia sat down in the pilot seat. "That's why I need Sauries. I don't know everything that might pose a problem for us. Some things that are potential problems can seem benign. This is her tenth trip with me. She has interacted with the animals. She has insights that could spot a threat that even I might miss. If you expect me to be responsible for all these people, then I need her at my side, being an extra set of hands and eyes, at all times."

The commander did not look happy, but he vacated the seat. Sauries slid into his place without saying a word, at least not until the engines were running and no one else would be able to hear them.

"I didn't realize I was so needed."

"You're not." Alhia punched the throttle, sending them into the air. "You're just the only person I can stand listening to."

She smiled before turning away from him. She played her part, diligently watching the landscape below them. If anyone looked up, she was doing exactly what he said he needed her for. He had been landing close to the herd but this time chose a spot far away. He hoped to further discourage them by making it strenuous. Then he stood up and addressed the group.

"Even with the gene mutations I've done, these are still wild animals. They act on instinct, not reason and logic like we do, so there is no way to know what they will do next. They are five times our size. Their hooves are very sharp. We've had moons to observe and interact with these beasts, and still don't know everything that can trigger an outburst from them. I recommend staying back from the animals, even keeping something between you and them of you can."

When everyone eyed the door like it like it might not be enough to protect them, he figured he had said enough. He grabbed his equipment bag and headed down the ramp Sauries had lowered while he spoke. She was right behind him with another bag of supplies. But when he stopped at the bottom to count heads, so he could keep track of how many people were wandering around, the ramp was empty. No one even stood at the door. All of them were plastered to the windows, content with watching everything from the safety of the aircraft.

He shrugged, and headed off to do his job. There were new calves, which meant there were new mothers to track down. There were suddenly seven cows to milk, so it took longer than normal.

"I was surprised to see Kolpos on this trip and not Yosheia. I thought it would have been the other way around," he said as they crossed the field.

"I may have pressured them to set an example for the rest of the crew," she admitted, with a smirk, and then held out a hand towards him.

"What?" He looked down at her arm in confusion.

"Why don't you hand me some of those bags? The cows are used to us, and I think I'll be a lot more useful at their backside than rubbing their ears."

Once again, he was surprised at her willingness to help. As much as he wanted to tell her no, his legs ached at the idea of even more time hunched up. He gave her a couple of bags. "Thank you."

He watched her walk over to the nearest cow with milk dripping from her udder. It seemed she had been watching him, because she knelt down, cupped the bag over the teat and started squeezing. It took a couple tries, but milk soon squirted into the container. She looked up at him and smiled. He nodded, then turned around to find his own cow.

When he was done, he stood up, stretched his back and wiped the sweat from his forehead. Standing in the middle of the herd was the closest he'd come to being alone since leaving his quarters that morning. He took a second to enjoy that. He was used to being ignored and isolated. To suddenly be the center of attention was overwhelming.

Sauries' head popped up ten steps away. She looked as tired as he felt. He gave her a smile, grateful to have her. She was, obviously, the only crewmember willing to get her hands dirty milking. She was also comfortable talking to people when he wasn't. When their work was done, they packed up their gear and headed back to the ship.

"Look," she pointed to the side of the shuttle. "No faces in the windows."

"I wonder where they are."

He looked around, to see if any of them had exited the craft when they weren't paying attention. He didn't see anyone or any signs that they had come out. They climbed the ramp to find bodies lying every which way. A couple people sat up. One stood. A few were sound asleep.

"Is that the milk?" Gomesi asked.

"Yes." Alhia turned immediately to the storage cabinet, and stowed the gear, bags of milk and all. Then he did something he had never done before. He locked the door.

"Don't we get any?" Ophis put up his hands in emphasis.

"You will when Halis determines we have enough to share amongst the entire crew again." Sauries explained. "We don't want anyone to feel like they've been left out."

"So we came all the way out here for nothing?" Teres shook his head.

"You got to see what is involved in the collection process." Alhia made his way to the cockpit and ignored any further comments.

***

Alhia tentatively approached the waterline, sure he would find a scene similar to the day before. To his surprise, all was quiet. No one was visible from below the surface. Maybe word had gotten out how boring his work really was and everyone else had given up their silly idea of joining him. After a quick surge of water through his jets, he erupted out of the transition pool and plopped down on the chilly ledge. His smile faded when he heard the murmur of voices from the hall. With a groan, he kept his head down and went about his stretching routine.

At least no one rushed him. He worked every muscle group from head to toe. When he couldn't procrastinate any longer, he headed down the corridor, past the line of crewmen and scientists. Everyone stayed in line as he walked by. No one called out to him. No demands were placed. He was thinking things might be all right after all. That was, until he heard the quiet comments that were being said.

"The crew that went yesterday said it was boring," Ferox stood tall, leaning his head back against the bulkhead.

"If that's the case, should we waste a whole day doing this?" Miliaris looked back and forth at the others around her for a response.

No, you shouldn't, Alhia thought, but kept the comment to himself because he knew it would not be received well. He kept walking, with his head tilted away from the bystanders.

"I think they all got fresh milk and are just waiting for us to give up our seats so they can go out a second time and get more." Tarpon crossed his arms over his chest.

"No." Miliaris shook her head. "They said all the milk was brought back."

"That's what they said, and I know some was. But that doesn't mean that was all the milk. Who knows how much was really collected? I'm not giving up my seat. I need to see what's really going on out there," Tarpon said.

The geneticist stopped at the shuttle entrance and waited. He knew Sauries or someone higher ranking than her would soon be there to bring military order to the flight.

"I heard they never got out of the shuttle," Ferox added.

"I'm sure it was boring sitting in there for most of the day," Tarpon responded. "We're not going to be that foolish. We will all get out and see what's really happening."

Everyone stopped talking when they heard footsteps approaching. The military members stood at attention, as the captain walked by. He gave a brief nod to the people standing in line, and stopped to chat with one of the enlisted chaps. Then he walked up to the leader of the mission.

"So are we ready to go?"

"Well… Um…"

Before Alhia could explain, noise drew everyone's attention back towards the transition pool. Sauries made her way towards them with the uncoordinated steps of someone who had rushed through the stretching process.

"Sorry I'm late. I had to finish my log submissions. Is everyone ready to go?"

The CO gave the lieutenant a disapproving look but didn't say anything. Instead he turned around and led everyone into the shuttle. He went straight to the front row in the passenger compartment and sat down. He had heard about what had happened to his second-in-command the day before and wasn't going to go through that embarrassment. It was better to let everyone think he chose to sit in the back.

All the chatting had stopped. Everyone filed on board and took a seat. Sauries offered to help the scientist put away the gear, but he saw how much standing hurt her. He told her to go ahead and get in the cockpit. He closed the rear hatch, walked past the now-quiet passengers and started the preflight check list. He took his time, double-checking each item on the list. He was going to make sure everyone saw just how wearying it was to hang out with him.

By the time he landed, they were no longer being silent. Wisps of conversations drifted up to the front of the plane. When he finished shutting down the engines, and went back into the cabin, he saw the captain was the center of the conversation. He should have known; the officer was always jabbering to someone.

Alhia repeated the same speech he had the day before, making sure everyone was aware of the dangers they were about to face. Some of them had the same reaction as the last group, looking absolutely terrified.

Tarpon straightened his back, sitting up taller. “That’s fine. We don’t need to get up close and personal with the animals. But we don’t have to stay inside here, either.”

Many of the others agreed with him, but not all looked convinced. The geneticist gathered his gear while Sauries lowered the ramp. The crew stuck to their word, and all filled down the ramp as soon as it was safe. Sauries and he were the only ones inside as he turned to leave. He took a moment in the dark silence to take a deep breath and brace himself for the mayhem that was about to ensue.

The sunlight was bright as he stepped out. Their eyes were used to the light being filtered by water, so the brightness levels on the surface were always shocking. He blinked a couple times, and then saw that the ramp was clear. He headed down it with his assistant on his heels. Ferox and Miliaris stood at the bottom but quickly got out of his way. No one was more than ten steps from the security of the aircraft. Alhia never stopped; he just walked out towards the herd.

"They're being really brave," he said when they were out of earshot of the others.

She laughed. He smiled, happy that she got his humor.

The cow that had lost her calf was at the front of the group, waiting for them. Alhia knelt beside her, knowing it was arduous to stay crouched beside her and manually express that much milk. Sauries went over to the mothers with calves playing nearby.

When he was done with the first cow, he looked back at the others. He could only see seven wandering around the landing site. He looked around, but could not find the other three. He assumed they had gone back inside, since they were nowhere to be seen and he hadn't heard any screams.

By the time he was done, there were only two still outside and they were sprawled across the ramp, looking half asleep. As Alhia and Sauries approached, the waiting bodies leaned up on their elbows and blinked like their eyes were adjusting to the light.

"Is that all the milk?" Tarpon asked.

"Yes," the geneticist answered.

"I saw how much was brought to the galley yesterday, and it's the same amount." Ferox said.

Alhia rolled his eyes and walked up the ramp between them as Tarpon glared at the man lying next to him. Everyone else was inside, looking the same as to the group the day before. From the grumbling comments he heard as he stowed the gear, he assumed this would be the last trip anyone would be tagging along for.

Chapter Twelve

Alhia paused at the entrance to the galley. It used to be a quiet place where people would slip in, get something to eat and then head back out again. In the last few days, that had changed. Now people stayed there to eat, and others hung around even when they weren't consuming food. He had skipped his last meal because of the congestion. His digestive track rumbled, letting him know doing that a second time would not be advisable.

With his shoulders pulled back, he swam into the room. Everyone turned and looked when he did. He was sure he could feel the water pressure increasing with everyone's sudden movements, but that might have been in his head. With a gulp, he pressed on. Teres intercepted his path to the dispenser.

"I just wanted to say thank you for taking us all out there. It was very interesting to see."

"You're welcome."

The scientist moved around the petty officer, assuming the conversation was over. The young engineer pivoted around, though, and came up alongside him.

"So you really have to go out there and do that every day?"

"Yes."

The geneticist took a container from the stack and turned to the algae dispenser. That was when Halis came through the door to the back. The corners of her mouth immediately rose, and she rushed over to place herself between him and his destination.

"Do you really want to eat more of this, or do you want to see what else we have available?" She laughed at his confusion. "We are only required to eat algae when we don't have a protein source. You've given us the best source of protein there is; milk. So, now we can seek the out the rest of our nutritional needs from a variety of plants this sea offers."

Taking him by the arm, the head culinary expert led him over to the nets hanging from the bulkhead. She handed him a small net. Of course, he had seen food put out like this on his previous missions, but that had been so long ago, he had forgotten to even look for it.

"We have kelp, sea grass, and eel grass. And for a limited time, we have Aldrovanda; a carnivorous plant. You should try at least one, they taste quite exotic."

As she described the plant, she took a small piece out and handed it to him. It was tangy and crisp. He took another piece and put it in the bottom of his net to enjoy at the end of his meal. She then backed out of his way and let him select what else he wanted. All of the other items were things he had nibbled on during one excursion or another and nothing he needed to sample first. With his net full, he turned to leave.

"Where are you going?"

Halis swam between him and the exit. He looked around and realized most of the people in the room were looking at him.

"I was going to take this back to my quarters."

"We thought you would eat here." Teres was once again at his side. "That way we could talk to you."

Alhia never ate in the galley, something the crew would have noticed if they had been observant. Nor did he want to start now, yet everyone waited to see how he would respond. He wasn't used to this kind of pressure. It wasn't like he cared if these people really liked him or not. He did not come on the mission to make friends. If there had been only one or two crewman asking him to stay, he would have blown them off. But he was surrounded by people that seemed to genuinely want him to stay.

The scientist swam over to the bulkhead by the doorway and hung his net from a hook after extracting a long piece of eel grass. He bit off a chunk and began chewing. The algae didn't require mastication, so he took a moment to enjoy the sensation of breaking down fibers between his teeth.

"Do you really need to go out there every day to gather the milk?" Gomesi asked.

He waited until he was done chewing and swallowed before answering. "Yes, which is the same as it would be for the aquatic mammals if they produced milk. Any time you drink milk, someone must go out and manually retrieve it."

Everyone in the room nodded along with his answer. He looked around, waiting for another inquiry. When no one spoke up, he took another bite.

"Are you going to change the sea cows the same way you changed the ones on land and make them give us milk?"

This question didn't annoy him as much as the others. It was, after all, in his area of expertise. He was happy to help further along anyone's understanding of science.

"The genetic adaptions I did to the bovine were similar to the ones that were done to the whales before they were brought here. It seems life in the oceans of this planet is too hard and they had to change in order to survive. So forcing them to revert back would most likely be detrimental."

Only a few people nodded in response. The others had an expression like they weren't really listening. That was the response he got most often, so he was pleasantly surprised to have gotten through to as many as he had.

With the last of that piece of eel grass in his mouth, he avoided making eye contact with anyone while he chewed. He was able to eat while performing many of his routine tasks, but holding down a conversation while trying to consume food was annoying and ineffective.

"Are you going to make other species give us milk?"

Alhia laughed. Everyone was confused by his reaction, so he explained. "At this time, I have my hands full with the one herd. I would have to have additional workers to collect it if I were to increase production."

Suddenly everyone avoid making eye contact with him. It seems that while they were curious and enjoyed the fruits of his labors, no one was willing to assist in the work. He chuckled and pulled out a chunk of kelp out of his sack.

"Do you think you'll volunteer for another deep space mission after this one?" Tarpon asked.

Alhia took a bite, deliberately giving himself time before he had to answer. It paid off. Others added their opinions, and a full-fledged discussion went on around him without him having to add to it. He noticed Diopus, the Master Chief from engineering, also listened without participating.

What started out as a reasonable conversation quickly turned to subjects the scientist had no interest in, and he was getting rather annoyed at the responses he heard. People with no scientific training whatsoever were speculating on subjects that should be left to the professionals. Before he could explain the folly of their ways, others spoke up, leading the conversation in another equally unlikely direction. Finally he had had enough. He took his net from the hook and turned towards the passageway.

"I have things in my lab I must attend to." He explained as he turned to go.

Suddenly, Halis was there in his bubble radius. He thought anyone near enough to disturb the air bubble he stirred up were too close. He backed up as she pressed closer, seemingly determined to keep him there.

He needed a polite reason to leave. He imagined his workbench, trying to think of a project he could offer as an excuse. The only things on the bench were the log books Lyblepis had left there.

"The biologist asked me to look over some logs for him, so I need to get back to work." He figured the young scientist would understand him stretching the truth, considering the circumstances.

Many grumbled, but they parted and let him leave. There were a couple of brief conversations in the passageways, but eventually he made it to the privacy of his lab. He hung the net from a hook, then rubbed his face. He was back in his sanctuary, the one place he didn't have to worry about interacting with others. He could feel his blood pressure lower and his body relax. He looked around the room and realized he had nothing to do but eat in peace.

"Hey," Miliaris said from the doorway. "I heard this was where you were at. I just stopped by to chat."

Bile rose in Alhia's throat. Slowly he turned around and saw her with a hand on each side of the door jam. She had the same smile she always wore; the one that made everyone question how she ended up a microbiologist. She was just too cheery to be taken seriously.

She had never been to his lab before, not even to pick up supplies or for a consultation. The only time they had interacted was brief encounters in the passageway, usually coming or going from a meeting. Now she thought it was alright to pop in and visit him? If he let her in, who else would want to follow in her example? This was something he needed to put a stop to immediately. He rushed over to the bench where the logs were still stacked on the corner.

"I have so much work to do." He bowed his head apologetically. "I really don't have time to socialize. I have this whole pile I need to get through."

"Oh." She smiled. "I didn't mean to disturb you. That looks like a lot of work."

"It is."

He nodded and picked up the first ledger. He watched her go over the top of the screen. He worried if he put down the information someone else would see he wasn't busy and want to talk, so he grabbed a piece of kelp and started reading. Pretty soon he was caught up in the information, and then shock by what was written.

***

Pain in Alhia's right hip woke him up. At first he was disoriented, then he realized the artificial current had carried him to the corner of the room. It wasn't the first time he had woken up there, and just like before, he was grateful he hadn't been carried out into the corridor. That would have been embarrassing.

He had fallen asleep reading the logbooks. Most of the entries were the tedious and mundane tasks that make up most of a scientist's life—all things that need to be recorded, no matter how trivial they seem at the time. But some of the notations had been completely unexpected.

The geneticist rushed over to the last one he had been reading. It was the final one, and he was almost finished with it. Then he checked the time, and was surprised it was already daylight. He had slept in after staying up so late. Sauries would be expecting him at the shuttle before long. Instead of heading out to meet her, he gathered up the logs. What he had discovered was too important to wait.

Since it was late in the morning, crewmen were coming in and out of the galley as he passed. Some of them wanted to speak to him. He missed the days of being a loner and pretty much invisible. He didn't make eye contact with anyone. He didn't respond to any of their salutations, swimming past them all as if the corridor were empty. He didn't stop until he got to the CO's stateroom.

"Captain? Are you in? There is something I must discuss with you."

This was not something he had ever done before, so he wasn't sure what the appropriate protocol was. How was he supposed to properly barge into the commanding officer's quarters when he wasn't expected? It was probably covered in the military training he had not attended. Come to think of it, it probably wasn't. Most likely, they were just told not to.

"Enter."

The outer chamber was empty. Alhia stuck his head around the corner, and saw no one was in that room, either. Then Yosheia came in from his sleeping area, motioning the scientist to join him.

"Lyblepis brought me the old log books from his department, hoping the information inside might be useful. I read them last night, and you need to know what's in here."

The captain's posture and expression were instantly attentive. He looked like the man that had started the mission. His posture was straight and the tired lines around his eyes were gone.

"It seems the lifeforms that were seeded on this planet, the large black and white dolphins in particular, are very aggressive," the scientist explained.

The officer smiled and used a tone like he used explaining things to a young crewman fresh out of boot camp. "There is a reason carnivores are chosen. Their predilection to kill makes them ideal protectors. It can seem very gruesome when they kill fish, but this is the way it's been done for a millennium on dozens of planets."

The geneticist dipped his head. "This is more than that. I understand their need for food. I read multiple accounts of witnessed killings where the carcass was not eaten. There are also documented cases of the orcas targeting other mammals. They were supposed to be clearing out the native species, not the engineered animals brought here with them."

The commander's brow pulled down with concern. "It is not unheard of for a few animals to go rogue. The act of a few individuals does not represent the whole of the species."

"These accounts describe entire pods hunting in this fashion, not just one or two animals."

Yosheia swam back and forth across the room. "These accounts do sound disturbing, but you're talking about the most intelligent species brought to this planet. Their vocabulary has enough overlapping words with ours that we should be able to reason with them."

"That is exactly what the biologists thought. The first individuals to approach the pods were killed instantly. Even in groups, they were slaughtered."

"Why did I not hear about this?" the captain demanded. "All reports I received were that the deaths were caused by predators native to here."

Alhia looked down with slumped shoulders. "Throughout the logbook are references to the biologist's guilt over the animal's behavior. They viewed the brutality as the result of their own shortcomings. Then they viewed every unsuccessful attempt to fix things as another failure. The notes from the last few missions revealed their intention was to not come back. They would rather die than explain what had happened."

The captain didn't immediately respond. He stared into the corner while he gathered his thoughts. Before he could say anything, the door opened and the XO walked in.

"I'm sorry for interrupting. I had assumed you be in the galley having breakfast at this time. I had just come in to get the list of crewmembers permitted to swim today."

"Hold off on that. There is something you need to hear first."

Everything was repeated for the commander.

"So all the restrictions on swimming here were put in place because of deaths that were planned-out suicidal trips past the bio nets and not random animal attacks like we were led to believe?"

"It seems that is the case." Alhia was glad to finally get his point across.

"Which means we can lift the restrictions on swimming as long as they stay in the sea." The executive officer let the corners of his mouth curl up. It was a strange sight on the man that normally wore a stern expression.

"Before we rush out, we need to figure out how we are going to present this to everyone. I don't want this information to get out to anyone else. No one outside this room will ever hear of it, so we need a plausible reason for the change in policy." The captain had his arms crossed.

"You could tell them an upgrade was made to the bio nets, and another sweep on the sea confirmed it is free of predators." Alhia raised his eyebrows as he made the suggestion.

"Are they really supposed to believe you've had time to do all that?" Kolpos asked.

"Of course not." The scientist shook his head. "Everyone knows I'm on land all day."

"I'll make an announcement that Kolpos took the initiative and made it happen."

The second in command was shocked. "Captain, that is a lot of credit to bestow on me."

Yosheia put a hand on the lower-ranking officer's shoulder.

"I'm retiring after this mission, so it doesn't matter what anyone thinks of me. Your career has been tarnished by what has happened here. I am just doing what I can to keep you in good standing when we leave."

The commander looked down and blushed. "Thank you, sir."

Chapter Thirteen

When Alhia returned to the galley, he was on the heels of the two senior officers. The crewman that usually approached him stayed back and eyed the trio coming in, but the scientist didn't want people to think he was with the command. So he swam over, grabbed a piece of kelp, then made a loop back towards the entrance. Once he was near the way out, he took a bite. That was when the pipe announced the all-hands meeting.

It was better being on this side of the room and not at the front with everyone looking at him. But there was a downside to being part of the crowd. It was normal that first people in the room went to the far side, making room for others to come in. If someone bumped into you, it was common courtesy to give leeway. He refused to be polite. He was backed against the bulkhead and would not be pushed into the corner. He was ready to bolt at the earliest opportunity, and wasn't going to let anyone get between him the way out.

So, when people coming in kept jostling him, trying to force him deeper into the room, he refused to budge. He pulled his shoulders back, locked eyes on the front of the room, and leaned into the current of the incoming crowd.

"Alhia, what's going on? Why are you ignoring me?" Sauries asked.

"Ignoring you?" He was surprised to see she was right next to him.

"I've nudged you three times to get your attention, and you haven't acknowledged me. You just keep staring straight ahead like I'm not even here."

"My apologies." He dipped his head. "It was completely unintentional. People entering were pushing me, expecting me to be like everyone else and shuffle to the center of the room. I had assumed your touch was just more of the same."

She nodded and rested up against the wall next to him. "Two all-hands meeting this close together is unheard of. Do you know what it's about?"

He was saved from having to lie by the captain asking everyone to be quiet. Not everyone heard. A few stray remarks rang out in the sudden quiet.

"What's this all about?"

"It's too early for the announcement we have cheese."

"Has the mission been terminated?"

"No. No." Yosheia finally got everyone's attention. "Everyone needs to calm down. I'll be happy to tell you what's happening as soon as everyone's quiet." He paused. When nothing else was said, he continued. "I know we recently had a monumental change, but that doesn't mean we are willing think that things are good enough. We are still working tirelessly to continue terraforming the planet and bring a successful end to our mission. I have kept our most current attempts a secret, knowing how devastating our previous failures have been to morale. While I hoped the steps we took would bring a positive change to our situation, I didn't want to get everyone's hopes up. But now, we have good news. Since this was all Kolpos' idea, I'm going to let him explain it."

A murmur swept through the crowd as the other man came forward. Then they quickly grew silent again, wanting to know what he was going to say. He was not the eloquent speaker the captain was. He cleared his throat and fiddled with his hands before finally looking up.

"After a long analysis, we were able to determine how to strengthen the bio net. I implemented the upgrades, and then scanned the entire sea, including all coves and bays to ensure no predators were trapped inside. I'm happy to tell you that everything was successful, so we can lift all swimming restrictions."

At once, everyone in the room as talking. Kolpos had to raise his hand to get everyone to stop.

"As long as you stay in this sea and don't cross the bio net, it is safe to be out at any time even if you are alone."

After that, the officer couldn't be heard over the furor. Alhia looked down at Sauries. Her mouth hung open. It seemed she was the only one in the room rendered speechless. He moved around her to get to the door. She grabbed his arm to keep him from leaving.

"Are you going out to swim?"

"No. I have work to do."

She nodded and let her hand fall down to her side. He swam ahead of the crowd, then turned, heading in the opposite direction from them, assuming they would all head straight for freedom. He did wish he could be at the front of the group, with cool water over his gills in search of the most isolated place he could find. But the cattle needed to be milked, and he knew everyone depended on him to get them protein.

Alhia dillydallied in his lab until he thought everyone else would have left the ship. When all was quiet, he finally ventured out. The passageways and common areas were empty. While it was disappointing to have to continue tending the livestock instead of out exploring on his own, at least he had the ship to himself. Nobody stopped him to ask him the same question that had the day before. There wasn't going to be a line of people to join him on the flight. He swam through the corridors with a little extra sway in his glide, enjoying the solitude.

As he came around the last bend, he saw two feet hanging in the transition pool. He immediately assumed it was Diopus, thinking that an engineering emergency was the only thing that would keep anyone on board. Interacting with the chief engineer wouldn't be so bad; he was a man of few words. The scientist broke the surface prepared to give a brief nod to the other male. Air and water spurted from his gills when he realized it was Sauries sitting there. She stopped stretching and laughed at him.

"What are you doing here?"

She tilted her head to the side. "The same thing you are. The animals need to be milked."

After pulling himself out of the water, he said, "The responsibility is mine. You don't have to come. You should be out celebrating with the others."

"I'm not here just to help you," she admitted with a demure grin.

His arm that had been high over his head dropped down to his side. "How so?"

"During our commute, I've paid attention to the scans of the water below us. There is a deep section on the far side of the sea. It would take me until nightfall to swim there. But with the shuttle, we would have plenty of time to harvest milk and still have a few hours of daylight to explore the depths."

"That makes me feel better." He resumed limbering up. "I would have felt guilty if you were being altruistic, but I think this arrangement will benefit us both."

The geneticist stood with his first smile that felt natural. As much as he had wished for the crowds to go away, it was nice to not be alone. There was a lot of work to do, and having someone to share the load with would make it go much faster.

They watched the monitors as they flew out. Sauries was right. There was a deep section even larger than the one everyone frequented on the west side of the Catenata. He pushed the throttle, suddenly in a hurry to get everything done so they could get back to the spot they had just marked.

Two new calves had been born during the night, giving them even more cows that needed to be milked. His excitement faded as he saw how much work loomed in front of them.

"Well, we might as well get started." She marched into the herd.

They did not talk after that, nor did they take time to meander among the animals. They both went from one udder to another, filling bags and stacking them in the tote. Their efforts paid off. The sun was just past its zenith when they finished up the last two cows.

She shoved everything into the storage locker while he started the engines. She didn't bother locking it, but did set the temperature controls to keep the space cool. That was something they usually never bothered with when they were flying straight back to the Catenata. This time, she hoped, they would not be getting back until after dark.

***

He brought the craft down on the water's surface. Gentle waves made it rock. He programmed the propulsion system to maintain the current position, despite the current pushing them. They both got up and went to the back. He lowered the ramp until it just touched the tops of the swells.

"I've set us down in the exact center of the trough. Do you want to swim east or west?"

"Which way is better?" she asked.

He shook his head. "The whole point of this was to make them as equal as possible. Hopefully they are about the same."

She thought for a moment. "Except there is a large river that flows north into the sea east of here. That will bring some exciting currents with it." She smiled at him. "Do you mind if I go that way?"

"If you had not wanted to do this, I would still be hunched down beside a furry beast, so please go whichever way you wish." He looked out over the sea. "When do you want to meet back here? Technically, all swimming restrictions have been lifted; we could stay here all night."

"I don't know." She grimaced. "I don't feel right about staying this far away from the Catenata. What if something happens? I need to be around to help if there are any mishaps today. How about we meet back here at twilight?"

"Sounds good."

After flashing a big grin, Sauries ran down the ramp, jumped, and somersaulted into the water. She resurfaced laughing, waved at him, then disappeared into the depths. He walked to the edge, pushed up with his legs, flipped over, and entered the water head first, barely making a splash. He used the outer controls to raise the ramp, sealing the shuttle. Once it was secure, he headed off in the opposite direction.

He followed the light rays down as they danced between the water molecules. He had spent so long in the shallows, his instinct was to slow down before he hit bottom, though he had seen the measurements and had a long way to go before he ran into any obstacles. He jetted water, propelling himself even faster towards the dark waters below him.

Eventually, he did find sand and rocks, and turned to swim along the bottom. An octopus caught his attention, so he took some time to watch it. The gangly creature was trying to balance two rocks together and hide in the space between them. Unfortunately, he was larger than the cavern he created, so every time he got his body and all his legs inside, it would push one of the rocks over. It was comical to observe as the futile efforts were repeated over and over again. The animal still persisted as Alhia finally swam away.

It felt so good to have nowhere to go, and nothing to do. He swam as hard as he could, turning right and then swaying left, and still had vast emptiness as far as he could see. Eventually, the light waves no longer filtered down into the water. He knew this meant the sun neared the horizon.

With leisurely strokes, he made his way up to the shuttle just as twilight began. His approach brought him to the cockpit windscreen. Everything was dark inside, just as he had left it. He made a lap around the craft. Sauries wasn't back. That was to be expected. It was their first chance in a long time at real freedom, and she was bound to take advantage of every moment of it.

Alhia swam circles around the shuttle. When he got tired of that, he went under the craft. All the while, his eyes swept the area, looking for her return. Eventually, the light faded and the stars and the planets in the sky became visible. Still she had not come back.

It had been her idea to come back at twilight, so she should be there. He didn't want to assume the worst. It was an area they had never been before, so maybe she just underestimated how long the trip back would take. If the currents had changed, it might take twice as long as the swim out had. To pass more time, he counted each individual star as it appeared.

By the time the Milky Way was bright in the sky, he could no longer stay calm. What if they had been wrong to assume it was safe to swim again? They had told everyone another scan had been done, but that was just so they didn't have to admit the last few deaths had not been accidents. In reality, the sea had not been scanned since they set up the bio net. What if the safety measure had failed and predators had slipped through? Or what if there was a new threat they hadn't encountered before? He was unable to wait any longer.

His first impulse was to rush out and look for her, but he knew that was not practical. It would take him too long to cover everywhere she might have gone. If she were injured and bleeding, she would not be able to wait that long.

He climbed into the cockpit, and powered up the ship. It took a moment for the systems to fully come online. The auditory alarm pinged that there was a lifeform approaching the stern. The first scan revealed it to be about the same size as him. The second, more detailed scan showed it was Sauries. She swam slowly. He assumed she was injured. Blood would draw in predators. He did a low-resolution scan out as far as he could; nothing was following her.

There was not anything more the sensors would be able to tell him. He rushed aft and lowered the ramp until it was submerged in the water. He could see her on the surface. Her upper extremities pulled her towards the shuttle, but she barely advanced with each stroke. He grabbed the remote steering controls, and maneuvered closer to her. When the sound of the engines gearing up carried through the night air, she rolled over on her back and floated, knowing he was coming to her.

As he approached, he could see how exhausted she was. To his relief, there was not any blood in the water. Whatever had happened had not punctured her skin. He stopped the shuttle's forward momentum while she was still out of reach; he did not want to risk hitting her with the ramp. She rolled over and gave him a weak smile. She reached out but didn't have the strength to lift her arm. He dove into the water, and surfaced right next to her.

"What happened?" He lifted her up onto the ramp.

"Nothing."

She rolled up the incline out of the water. Her feeble attempt to sit up only ended up with her loosing half the ground she had gained. Alhia pushed himself out of the water and knelt beside her. He immediately palpated her extremities, even though she tried pushing him away.

"What do you mean 'nothing' happened? This level of exhaustion is an indication of shock."

She gave up trying to fight him and lay back on the hard metal. He would see for himself that she had no injuries. He checked her from head to toe, being extra thorough assessing her skull. Eventually he gave up, leaned back and just looked at her.

"Nothing happened," she repeated. "I didn't interact with any other lifeforms. I didn't get knocked into any rocks. I had a wonderful swim. Everything was going great when I turned around to come back. Then I noticed I was a little tired. There was a current and I was swimming into it, but it really wasn't that strong. The further I went, the worse it got. Eventually it took everything I had just to maintain forward momentum. I guess I've gotten out of shape spending so much time on the ship."

Alhia picked her up and carried her to a bench seat at the back of the shuttle. Before he let her lay down, he checked her back for bite or sting marks. There were none.

"Are you sure you weren't attacked by a jellyfish or an eel? They're small, so you might not have seen them."

"I'm sure." She laid back. "I would have felt either of those. This was just a very gradual loss of strength."

He set the air temperature a little higher than normal and gave her some algae. "Eat this, just in case your blood glucose level has dropped. I'm going to get us back so I can get you to sick bay."

"Thank you, but you're blowing this out of proportion. I'm sure I'll be fine."

He closed the ramp and gave her a disbelieving look. "Relax. I'll have us back soon."

"I will on one condition: don't call ahead to the ship. I'm fine. Really. I don't want a medical team waiting for me when we dock. If you really think I need to be checked out, I will go to the clinic with you, but I don't want this made into anything more than what it really is."

"Okay. I promise. You rest, and we will see how you're doing when we're back on the Catenata."

He knew he was too distracted to pilot, so he set the computer to take them back, which ended up being a good thing, since he felt like he was looking back into the cabin more than he was looking through the windshield. Not that there was anything to see. He couldn't see her over the rows of seat backs. He had to assume that since she didn't say anything, she was doing fine.

As the shuttle coupled with the main ship, Sauries forced herself up into the sitting position. She was still tired, but it wasn't the exhaustion she had felt getting out of the water. By the time Alhia made it back to the passenger compartment, she managed a smile. He offered her a hand, but she ignored it and stood up next to him. He was watching her closely, so she willed herself not to wobble. When he finally looked up at her face instead of studying her body, she let out a pent-up breath and relaxed.

"I told you, I'm fine."

"We'll see," was all he said in reply.

He continued to examine her as they went to the transition pool. She eased herself into the water and was grateful to have it take her weight. Once he was in the water, she swam a couple of laps around him.

"I told you, I'm fine. I'm not going to medical."

"Are you sure?"

"Yes."

"Well, I'm going to see you to your quarters."

He let her swim ahead of him, since he was carrying all the milk they had collected. She was a little slower than usual, but he had to admit that wouldn't warrant medical attention. They made it through two full twists of the corridor before they ran into their first shipmate. They were both surprised, assuming everyone would be out swimming. By the time they made it to her quarters, they had seen two more.

"I'm fine." She grasped his hand.

The color had returned to her cheeks, and she looked a lot better than she had in the sea. He took her word that she was all right, and headed towards the galley. He needed to stow the day's collection in the cold storage.

He was surprised to see even more people there. He could understand being hungry after an exerting day, but why didn't they just find something fresh to eat? Curiosity overcame his aversion to people when he saw Ferox in the group.

"What's going on?"

The young scientist shrugged. "It felt weird being out there after dark. I figured I'd let someone else be the first to do it. You know, make sure it's safe."

Alhia nodded, and then went on to the back room. It had been more than ninety years since any of them had experienced the water at night. It made sense for them to be a little leery. He just hoped that someone was in fact overnighting off the ship, so they could report back to the others that it was safe.

Chapter Fourteen

Alhia was startled awake. He opened his eyes to Kolpos' face and instinctively jumped back. The sleeping hammock swung backwards from his momentum, then swung forward again. The second in command swam backwards out of the way, not looking happy to be there. None of the command had been in his lab before. The X.O. waking him up didn't make sense. This was not a courtesy the officers offered—thankfully. He found their strict schedules confining.

The scientist slid out of the hammock. Kolpos backed away from him as he did. His eyes focused on the movement, at first, then noticed two more crewmen waiting by the door. The Catenata had no need for a full-time security force; there just weren't enough incidents to justify an additional crewman. It was well known that the two just inside the hatch had the collateral duty to fill that position on the rare occasion it was needed.

"What?" The geneticist stammered. "What's going on? Is something wrong?"

"You could say that." Kolpos finally spoke. "Why didn't you bring Sauries to sick bay as soon as you returned? You know protocol requires immediate medical attention when someone shows any sign or symptom of being exposed to a foreign pathogen."

"Of course I know that." The scientist paused to remember all the events of the day before. "There was no exposure event. She told me she was just a little tired and didn't want to go to medical. Ask her. She'll tell you."

"That will not be possible. She was unconscious last time I saw her."

"What?" Alhia steadied himself. "Where is she?"

"She is in sick bay, being treated."

Alhia rushed for the door, but both security personnel moved to block the hatch before he could get there. He stopped just short of colliding with the two. He stared at both in confusion, not understanding why they would keep him from going to her. He swung around to the officer.

"I need to see her."

"You will, soon enough." The commander moved aside to reveal the bundle they had brought into the lab. "First, I need you to put on this suit and mask."

The geneticist looked down at a biohazard suit. It had been a long time since he worn one, but he was familiar with the garment. "What? Why?"

"You were with Sauries when she was exposed. You will be quarantined with her."

"There was not an exposure."

The executive officer did not look convinced. He picked up the isolation gear and handed it to the other man. "Have you not spent the last few lunar cycles interacting with beasts?"

"Well, yes." The geneticist looked confused. "But nothing that has happened in the field could cause anyone to be ill. If there had been a pathogen released, everyone would have been exposed through the milk."

Kolpos briefly showed surprise, but then quickly went back to being expressionless. "You're right. I will need to get the milk supply contained as soon as I get you secured." He pushed the mask and suit into the other man's arms.

"Is this really necessary? Twenty crewmembers went out to the site with us, not to mention that everyone drank milk."

The XO swam up to a position where he could look down on the scientist. "Protocol says you must be quarantined until tests prove it is not necessary."

All three had their arms folded across their chest. It didn't seem like any of them were going to see logic. He gave up the fight and donned the isolation gear. Thankfully there was hardly anyone in the passageway to see him being escorted through.

When they turned into medical, Gomesi was in the first room. He was at the far wall with a list in one hand and a bottle in the other. He didn't look surprised at the strange group coming in. He stayed where he was and just watched the others pass into the next room. Alhia expected to see the psychologist laying on the exam table, but it was empty. Velifer was on the far side of the room, running an analysis.

"Straight into the back?" Kolpos asked.

"Yes," the doctor responded without turning around.

The hatch on the far wall that had been opened before now stood closed. The X.O. swam ahead and spun the handle. He stayed behind the second door as the civilian entered into the last room. As soon as he was through, the door was sealed behind him.

There were four exam tables. Sauries was on the closest one. Alhia rushed over, asking if she were okay. The clumsy suit kept him from taking her hand. She didn't move, but her eyes fluttered open.

"I told them you were fine." Her voice was weak.

"What happened to you? You assured me you were feeling better."

"I was." She spoke slowly, flushing more water over her gills every couple of words. "Just tired. Went to sleep. Woke up here. Sensors in bed… picked up… high fever."

"We need you to take off your suit and get into bed."

He waved off the comment, knowing the voice through the speaker came from Velifer, who would be observing everything in the room and able to see the gesture.

"Did you seize?"

"I don't know." Answering questions added to her exhaustion. "I was unconscious."

The doctor barked more orders, but Alhia ignored them. The sickly figure in front of him had his full attention. Most of their communication was through body movement and facial expressions. The words were only a small part of it. With her only able to speak, he had to pay close attention to catch everything.

"Were you exposed to something when you were swimming by yourself?"

"No."

"What caused this, then?" He asked her as much as he asked himself.

"Don't know." She closed her eyes for a moment, then slowly opened them again. "They're running tests."

This time when she closed her eyes, she didn't open them again. Her cheeks were gaunt and her color had faded. He finally turned around and complied with the instructions he'd been given. He took off his isolation suit and put it in the bin marked for decontamination. He put on the sensors that would track his vitals, then stretched out on the table closest to Sauries.

He had just gotten a full night's rest, so he wasn't tired. He watched her for a while, but she was sound asleep. Eventually, he couldn't lie there any longer. An observation screen allowed him a view of the other side of the hatch. In the camera angle, he could see a crewman being treated for a minor injury. He watched as the wound was dressed and the patient was released. When Velifer was done, he noticed the scientist in the middle of his screen.

"How long have you been there?"

"Long enough to see you treat that abrasion."

The doctor gave him an exasperated look. "You can't stay there and watch what I do. My patients deserve some privacy."

Alhia nodded. "I need something to occupy my time."

"Well, then you can be my nurse and take care of Sauries. That way I won't have to go through decon every time she needs something."

"I'll be happy to when she wakes up. What do I do in the meantime?"

They were interrupted by a timer. The doctor went over to the analyzer and looked at the results. "Damn."

"What is it?" Alhia had his hands up against the monitor, trying to get close enough to see.

"Nothing." The doctor finally turned away from the results with a scowl. "Everything came back negative. We have no idea what is going on."

"What can I do? Let me come out there and help you."

"Did you not hear what I said?" The medical officer stared at the camera lens on top of the monitor. "A fever is the body's reaction to an infection, and we just ruled out all known pathogens. Whatever is causing this is something we've never seen before, hence the quarantine. If we don't have a way to fight this, we need to minimize our losses."

The severity of the situation finally sunk in. The one person on the ship he could stand interacting with lay seriously ill behind him. She might be contagious, and he was trapped in the room with her.

Oddly, he wasn't worried. He doubted that bacteria, fungus or any other single-celled organism would have found her first when he'd been out in the field longer. He didn't think it was possible she could have come in contact with anything the he himself hadn't also been wading through, yet he wasn't feeling any symptoms. So, either he was immune or what was going on with her was not caused by a microbe. He just hoped that whatever caused her illness wasn't his fault. Though he was the reason she was traipsing around on land, so most likely it was.

"Well, I have to do something."

"I need more samples. Do you think you can get those?"

"Samples?" Alhia suddenly wasn't so sure of himself. "From Sauries?"

"Yes, of course from her. I will eventually need them from you, too. For right now, I'm focusing on her since she is the one that's symptomatic."

"As you should." Alhia nodded. "I was hesitant because I've studied getting samples from all species, I've never collected them from our own."

"There is a first time for everything."

The comment wasn't exactly reassuring, but it was correct. It did make sense for him to perform the task. He turned around and started looking through cabinets to see where everything was stored.

To ensure efficiency, there were duplicates of all the testing equipment inside the quarantine area. Alhia gathered what he needed and set it all on the tray next to her bed. She was sound asleep, completely unaware of what he was doing. He sanitized the area of her arm he was about to stick the needle into, and realized it was the first time he had initiated physical contact with her. She had nudged him a few times when he wasn't paying attention, but neither of them had laid hands on the other. Now he was prepared to pierce her skin and take bodily fluids from her.

He had to stop thinking of her as the one person that helped him with all the field work and look at her as just another mammal. This was no different than collecting samples from a porpoise. Easier, because her extremities offered more locations where veins were accessible.

Alhia was very cautious, only relaxing when she slept through everything he did. From then on, it was like being in his lab. The blood was separated into different components and each part was analyzed. He placed tissue samples under the microscope and found plaques; well defined patches of cells with degeneration and lysis.

Chapter Fifteen

Sauries' body labored to force water over her gills and her oxygenation levels continued to drop despite all the work she was doing. Alhia was continually running back and forth between the machines analyzing the samples and her bedside. They had already run every test they could think of, and none of them had shown why she was sick. They had tried multiple things to counteract the symptoms, but without being able to address what was causing them, all they were able to do was add a little more time to her life.

He held algae up to her mouth. Before she had eaten some, but now she did not respond. A sensor chimed, and he looked at the monitor to see what was going on. Her heart rate and blood pressure were running the same as they had been since he came into the room. Her oxygenation levels were still concerningly low, but they hadn't dropped in the last few minutes. Then he looked at her temperature. Those numbers were in red and had suddenly risen.

"There is a temperature-regulating blanket in cabinet two. Can you please put it over her and set it to cold?"

He nodded to the camera and the doctor giving orders from the other room, then retrieved the item. He stretched the reflective material over her and set it to counter the spike in her fever. Her eyes fluttered open as he worked above her. She gave him a weak smile, and then her eyelids were once again too heavy to hold up.

He turned around to see Miliaris smiling on the monitor. Just when he was ready to snap at her that this wasn't a moment to be happy about, he realized he had never seen her without the smile. Instead of saying anything he would probably regret, he made sure the blanket complete covered Sauries, suddenly feeling like she was exposed on the table.

"How are things going?" The microbiologist tilted her head to the side.

"Not well." He looked down as he turned around to face the camera. "She is not responding to anything we've tried."

"I heard she was very ill." She tried to look somber, but still had a small grin. "I might know some tests that you haven't tried, or at least will be able do some of the testing so you can see to her other needs."

"I have already run every test I can."

She shrugged, and flashed her dimples. "I might have equipment that is not here. Do you have extra samples I could scan?"

"Yes." He nodded and then went to the shelf. "I would normally tell you not to bother, but I don't know what else to do." He placed the fluid samples in the connection tube, and sealed the door on his side. "How are things going out there?"

"Everything is going great." She gave the sign of gratitude, then opened the tube from her end. "Everyone is very excited to have open swimming again. The passageways are empty, since people are brave enough to stay out overnight, now."

"So there haven't been any problems?" He raised his eyebrows.

"No." She gathered the samples and put them in a tote to take back to her lab. "The upgrades Kolpos did are fantastic. I think the whole crew would have gone crazy without him." Her eyes flickered over his shoulder. "I will rush these specimens and focus on tests that are not normally used in medicine."

"Thank you. I hope you find something, anything that will help us."

She bowed, then made her way out. He watched her go and sat there staring at the screen. He had been confined to the small room for longer than he wanted to think about, and he stared at the space being recorded by the camera just because it was walls he hadn't memorized, floor he hadn't swam back and forth over.

With a sigh, Alhia went back to the chores awaiting him. He cleaned up what was left of their last meal, shaking his head at how little she had eaten. When everything was put away, he checked Sauries' monitors. Her vitals hadn't changed. Her fever hadn't abated. He palpated her forehead and cheek to confirm what the machines said. She did feel very hot, just as hot as she had before he put the cooling blanket on her.

She felt his touch, and turned into it. "Cold." She shivered, as if to show him what she meant. "Feel so cold."

"The cold is necessary," he explained, even though he doubted she paid attention to his response. "We need to bring your fever down. Your temperature is getting high enough to potentially cause brain damage. You're one of the few people that I don't find annoying. We can't have losing all that good sense you have."

She nodded at what he said, rolled over, curled up in a ball and continued to shiver. The material draped over her had slid down. He pulled it up over her shoulders and tucked it in around her. One hand slipped out with her pale fingers reaching out to him. He took her hand, and no longer concerned with the lights and beeping around him, he stayed there, letting her feel that he remained by her side.

"Alhia."

"Alhia."

He turned to the monitor, and was surprised to see Miliaris. Her expression was somber for the first time ever.

"Was there a problem running the test?" He tilted his head as he frowned.

"There were no problems." Her head hung down. "The machines all functioned properly."

"And what were your findings?" He let Sauries finger slide free of his and went over to the screen.

"Nothing." She looked directly into the camera. "Not a single microorganism that is not part of her normal flora. I have no idea what is causing this disease."

An alarm cut their conversation short. Sauries' blood oxygenation levels were below seventy percent, too low to maintain proper brain function. Miliaris was moved to the side, and Velifer appeared in her place.

"She has systemic edema. We need to disconnect her intravenous fluids."

Alhia looked at the camera with creased brow.

"Her body is swelling. She's retaining so much fluid, it's built up between the epithelial layers of her gills and the blood vessels below it. This prevents oxygen molecules from passing between them. We need to stop any more fluids from building up."

He stopped the drip and disconnected the tubing. It wasn't a procedure he was used to doing, but he managed to complete it. This was not going to be a quick change. He stood there, staring at her pallor, waiting for the machine to change. When the number finally climbed to seventy-one and the alarm stopped chiming, the exhaustion hit him. He went to the next exam table and collapsed.

***

Alhia woke up with a start. At first, what he saw didn't register in his brain. Two forms in bulky suits stood at the table next to him. Then he remembered where was, recognized the isolation suit he had had to wear here and realized they were working on Sauries. He sat up and turned towards them.

Velifer was on the far side, and looking at him. "I need you to stay where you are. There isn't anything you can do over here, anyway."

The scientist nodded and lay back down. He wished he could leave. He didn't want to watch what was going on. Though if his eyes weren't on Sauries and the efforts being done to save her life, then they were on the monitor screen that was showing that she didn't have a heartbeat.

They administered drugs, inserted a probe that applied direct electric current to the cardiac muscle and then even resorted to chest compressions. Despite everything they did, the numbers on the screen never changed. The psychologist on the table never revived.

Eventually they gave up. An isolation body bag was brought in, and her body was put into the cold storage area. Then the hatch was sealed and Alhia was alone in the room. He sat there for a while, hoping that he would wake up and find it was all a bad dream. But no matter how long he sat there, his only friend's body didn't reappear next to him.

The debris from their resuscitation attempt had been left where they had dropped it. When he couldn't stay still any longer, he picked it up. He knew not to put anything back in the cupboards, so he stacked what hadn't been used on a shelf. At some point, someone would disinfectant them with UV light so then they could be stored again without contaminating everything else in the cabinet.

He found the last set of samples that had been taken from her. If there was another case similar to this, they would be needed. He looked for a red biohazard bag, but couldn't find any. He ended up putting them in a plain white bag and setting them near the only exit.

Alhia was glad he hadn't gone into medicine. Being a nursemaid was the worst experience of his life. It might have been different if the patient weren't the one person in the crew he had a connection with, but he doubted it and hoped never to have a chance to find out. He turned around and looked at the empty exam table she had occupied. Suddenly, he didn't have the motivation to do anything else. He went to the other side of the room and lay down with his back to everything that had happened.

Chapter Sixteen

When the commanding officer swam into the clinic, the doctor snapped to attention. It was a formality the old man had grown tired of. He waved the junior officer out of the position of attention. The medical officer relaxed his shoulders, but only slightly. Worry lines still creased his face. The captain turned away, knowing that if he commented on what he saw, he would have to acknowledge his own grief. He looked around the room, hoping to find something to distract him. The room was bare. Everything had been put away. His eyes were drawn to the screen and the image of the body lying in the next room.

"What's *going on*?" Yosheia motioned to the screen.

Velifer shook his head. "Nothing. He's just laid there since we left the room."

"Is he sick?"

The concern he had been trying to ignore gripped him. The doctor swam over so they looked at the screen side by side. Now they both carried the same grim expression. "No. There has been no change with him. I think sleeping is how he's coping with what has happened."

The Captain nodded and looked at everything the camera showed. The quarantine area was exactly as he had last seen it. Everything was spotless and the only occupant didn't move.

"But he's stayed symptom free."

"Yes. We've seen no evidence she was contagious. Enough time has passed that any pathogen would have been through its incubation period and would have infected him."

There were a lot of questions that had already been asked, none of which had answers. It seemed nothing was going to explain why they had lost a very fine officer, just when they though the death count was totaled.

"But you need me to be the one to call it?"

The doctor nodded. "That is what protocol says."

He knew the doctor would have been thorough and made sure every procedure had been followed before getting the command involved again. But there was a reason he had to be the one to make the call. It would be on his shoulders if something went wrong, which meant he needed to verify that everything that had been done.

"We've not seen any other sign of sickness on board."

"No." The medical officer shrugged. "Everything indicates we rushed to judgement when we declared the quarantine. The only thing that keeps me from being completely convinced is that we don't know what killed her. Obviously, something we've never seen before made her sick. Really sick."

"Maybe she did have something, and your quick actions kept it isolated."

"Maybe, but then why didn't he get it?" Velifer pointed to the sleeping form on the monitor.

"Isn't that something you should explain to me?" the CO asked.

The lower-ranking officer held up his hands, showing they were as empty as his explanation. "Well, he's either proof that there was never a contagion, or he's immune to whatever was in there. Since we didn't identify a pathogen, everything points to the first theory."

Yosheia turned back to the screen. "Well, then, let's get him out of there."

The doctor opened both hatches, allowing the filtered and sanitized water from the room to mix with the current in the outer room. Yosheia led the way into the tight space and stopped with the rigid posture he assumed when performing any military function.

Alhia turned around with a shocked expression. "What are you doing?"

"Releasing you," the captain answered.

"You've gone through the prescribed time without any symptoms. Our protocol says you don't have to stay in here."

The doctor's words slowly sank in. He wasn't even sure how long he'd been confined. It had been many days, but how many he wasn't sure. He hadn't wanted to know while it was happening and wasn't sure if he wanted to know now that it was over.

The scientist looked around the room. His gaze stopped on the bed that Sauries had occupied. When he closed his eyes, he could still see her lying there. Not having any other option, he had chosen to sleep rather than stare at her last resting place. Suddenly he had an alternative.

He got up and looked around for anything he had brought with him. He realized he had come in with nothing, so he would leave empty handed. He headed past the two officers and headed towards the door. At the last moment, he grabbed the white bag. His plan had been to give it to Velifer, but his mouth didn't open. He didn't hand over the package. He held it tight up against his chest and went directly to his lab.

None of the equipment in medical analyzed DNA. There really was no reason. Everyone was screened for genetic disorders before they left their home world. Any abnormalities would prevent someone from doing off-world missions, so the few treatments they had for damaged chromosomes weren't available on a ship.

Alhia wouldn't be able to sleep until he had scanned Sauries' DNA. He hoped that he was fixated with this because it was his specialty and wouldn't find anything, but now that the idea was in his head, he couldn't let it go. At a minimum, he was just being thorough, doing the one test that hadn't been done already—a test he would have already done, if he hadn't been locked up. But he hadn't said anything, because he was scared of what the results would be.

Thankfully, he hadn't seen anyone else in the corridor. Everything in the lab was just as he had left it. He was glad to be back. Even though it was about the same size as the isolation room, he didn't feel trapped here, even when he turned around and shut the hatch. Usually the doors were left open. That way the water inside their rooms could circulate with the main stream in the passageway. Isolating yourself just led to stagnant quarters. Even knowing that, he sealed himself inside. He intended to stay there until he had the results. He wasn't completely sure that the quarantine had been cleared, and wanted to avoid others until he proved it to himself.

The vials used in medical were not compatible with his machine, so he had to transfer the samples to test tubes. The machines had to be prepared and programmed, but before long he had every piece of equipment in the room running. He swam from machine to machine, checking their status and trying to anticipate any problems that might come up. He realized the loop he made resembled the pacing he had done in isolation. Even with that knowledge, he continued the same path over and over again.

Eventually he became hungry. He had his own algae growth for times when he was involved in his testing and couldn't get to the galley. Since no one was around to eat it, it had grown to a few days' supply. He was halfway through his meal when the first machine chimed that it was done. He forgot about the food and rushed to the source of the sound.

The first time reading the results was a quick scan of the information. That was when the knot began to form in his stomach. He went back to the beginning, hoping that if he slowed down as he went back over it, he would find out he had misinterpreted it. Each line he read was painful, and it proved to be exactly as he had initially thought. In Sauries' DNA were markers he had used in the virus.

The next testing equipment finished. He was able to see each amino acid in sequence. He had worked with the DNA strand he had administered to the cattle so many times that he had memorized every piece of it. He was immediately able to see that the list in front of him was not an exact match. However, as reassuring as that should have been, there were too many consistencies for it to come from anywhere else.

Late into the night, Alhia studied the results. He fell asleep at the workbench, waking up in the wee hours of the morning. Seeing the lab when he opened his eyes filled him with hope. It was his first time not waking up in isolation, but he should have been in his hammock. As much as he wished the recent past had just been a nightmare, the closed hatch proved that it wasn't.

He looked down at the results from the night before. They were worse than what he had feared and left him with even more questions, ones he was determined to find a solution to. A quick glance at the display showed that it was not yet daylight.

He started down the passageway, but turned around and went back. Against protocol, he closed the door to the empty room. It just seemed prudent.

It was early, so no one else was out as he made his way to the top of the ship. He expected to see Sauries waiting for him at the transition pool and shook his head at the eerie feeling of being there all alone. He had spent most of his life isolated. He would quickly return to that being normal—at least he hoped he would.

The flight felt strange. He had no idea if he'd ever make the trip again. He watched the dawn give way to full rays of daylight just as he had for moons, and as much as he liked having a break from all the work and chaos that milking had been, he missed the routine he had become accustomed to.

He took a long loop around the valley before landing. He wasn't looking for anything in particular, nor did anything stand out .to him. He just wanted one last chance to take in every detail, worried that he might not be able to later. He was reassured to see that the river was strong enough to run year-round. He didn't have to worry about the cattle's water supply running out. There was enough grass to feed four herds. It was why he chose the place originally; the animals had everything they needed. Knowing that the land could sustain them without his intervention reassured him as he faced the real possibility that he would not be able to return.

Everything seemed exactly as it had the last time he was out there. The cows watched him as he exited the craft. When he'd been making daily trips, the animals hadn't even acknowledged him. The time away was enough to make them notice his arrival. They didn't run from him, but he imagined if they were left on their own long enough, they would.

The first cow he checked was the one that had lost her calf. He wasn't surprised to see her udders were almost back to the size they were before getting pregnant. Not being milked, she was drying up. Other than that, there was no other change. The animal looked healthy.

Next, he went to the ones who were nursing. Their udders were still the same size. They were still producing more milk than the calves could drink. Milk dripped down from their teats. He briefly considered collecting it, but that would just prolong the animal's over-production and no one would drink it. For so long he had craved the white frothy liquid, and now his stomach turned at the thought of it.

He took out the long syringe Velifer had given him at the start of the experiments. He numbed an area of the cow's hide over a blood vessel. He was no longer concerned about the animals being able to remember him inflicting pain on them. He just didn't want to get kicked when the needle punctured the skin. The animal didn't even notice as he stuck the vein and withdrew blood. With one quick motion he had withdrawn the equipment and set a clot over the hole.

He went back to the shuttle. He paused before going in and took one last look around. It wasn't so much that he didn't want to leave but rather that he didn't want to go back. He decided to take his time, detouring to the north and flying over the southern edge of the ice sheet. He made sure all daylight was gone before he clamped into the docking bay on the Catenata.

Chapter Seventeen

Alhia feared someone would be there to scold him for taking the shuttle, but the upper deck was empty as he walked out. The transition pool was a mirrored surface reflecting his image from below. He scowled and turned away. He was never one to care about his appearance, but suddenly it was more than that. He couldn't look at himself, because he would be looking at Sauries' killer.

He wanted to take off in the shuttle, go to the other side of the planet and never come back. He didn't want to see himself, nor did he want anyone else to see him—not that anyone else's judgement would be worse than his own. He knew he'd never be free of the guilt he bore. But at that moment he was more focused on finding out exactly what had happened.

He sulked through the passageway, glad that most of the crew had taken advantage of the ability to swim at night. One person was getting food in the galley. He stayed along the far wall, trying not to draw any attention to himself. Keeping his head down, he hadn't even seen who it was at the algae dispenser.

Back at the lab, Alhia ran the samples from the cattle through all the test he had put Sauries' blood through. He found the DNA he had encoded in the cells of the cows, which was what he had expected. He had already confirmed this before he had started collecting the milk. But unlike the initial results, this time there was something else in the strand. It was similar enough to the one he had made to be obvious that was where it had originated. Unfortunately, this was not the same as the one he had found in Sauries. He let all the tests run, collected all the data and confirmed there were two mutations from what he had designed.

The DNA he had constructed had been perfect. It simply added a few key components to make small alterations in the cellular make-up, tweaking the organism. The mutations were random, undoing his perfectly orchestrated amino acids he had strung together into something that served no purpose. The first change that had spontaneously occurred rendered the gene useless. It no longer expressed anything. It seemed the second transformation was even worse. Rather than just adding superfluous genetic material, it caused lysis of the cells it infected, killing everything it touched.

He knew what the next step was. He collected his own fluids, and ran them through the same process. For the first time in his life, he was truly nervous. He knew which machine would be complete first, and still he lapped the room, looking at the status of each piece of equipment until he heard the signal that one was done.

He quickly turned to the device blinking with waiting results, but then slowed down. What kind of results did he hope for? His instinctual reaction was to yen for neither of the mutations to be there. But there was another part of him that wanted to be infected with the same mutation Sauries had. If what he had done had killed her, he wanted it to eliminate him also. When he finally went to the screen, he immediately saw confirmation that the genetic markers were now in his DNA. Further results revealed that he had the first mutation, not the same as what the psychologist had carried.

He continued experiments into the next day. He discovered that having the first mutation made an organism immune to the second one. He was frustrated by the fact that after everything that had happened, there was no way he could simply die from what he had created.

***

With great trepidation, Alhia gathered all of his findings. Even though he was filled with shame and fear, he knew he needed to share what he had found. The medical shift started at dawn. So while it was still dark, he traversed the passageways. He managed to make it across the ship without laying eyes on anyone. He made himself comfortable in the waiting area.

Only moments later Velifer swam in, but from the treatment area, like he had been working for some time. His expression grew dark when he saw who was there ahead of him.

"Do not tell me you are now sick."

"No." The geneticist looked down. "But I have information I must share with you."

"If it's just information, it will have to wait."

Before he could offer rebuttal, the doctor rushed back where he had come from. Alhia followed. The captain was stretched out on an exam table, with closed eyes. He raised his head and looked up when he heard them come back in the room. He looked eerily like Sauries had after her swim. The scientist fell into place next to the doctor, all too familiar with what needed to be done.

"Are you sure you want to be here?" The medical officer frowned. "It seems, after everything we thought we knew about this, it is contagious after all."

"I am not concerned. I am immune."

The doctor was just about to start an intravenous line, but stopped with the needle in hand to look at the man on the other side of the table. "Is that an assumption based on not catching it while in quarantine, or do you have new insight?"

Alhia straightened his posture and stared at a spot on the wall over the other man's shoulder. "I have been running tests which show that the virions I produced to initiate the genetic alterations in the animals has mutated and infected us. Twice. The first change made the gene gibberish. It doesn't express anything, and is just unnecessary genetic material added into our sequence. The second transformation is detrimental. My results show that the presence of the first mutation prevents contracting the second."

Velifer's mouth hung open in an expression of horror. Alhia could not maintain his rigid stance any longer. His eyes went to the floor, not wanting to see that he would, in fact, be judged just as harshly by others as he did himself.

"What can we do?"

"If we were on one of the central planets, one where the aquatic mammals are engineered, they might be able to reverse what has happened. Any attempts I could make would just be repeating what I've already done, which would just end up with more mutations of more genetic material."

"We can't have that." The doctor shook his head as he prepared a bag of IV fluid. Then he looked down at the patient going in and out of consciousness, oblivious to what they were discussing. "We need to notify the command. Since the captain is incapacitated, we need to get Kolpos down here."

"Let's get Yosheia into quarantine." Alhia motioned to the door at the back of the room. "I don't want to be responsible for any more deaths than I've already caused."

The CO did not respond to being jabbed with a needle. Knowing he would be of no assistance, they moved the entire exam table into the isolation chamber. Alhia stayed with Yosheia to get everything situated while the officer made the necessary communications.

There was an odd familiarity as Velifer looked at the scientist attending the patient on the monitor. It was something he hoped to never see again. "The commander is on his way down. Come out here so we can brief him on the situation."

"I would prefer to stay in here."

"We're still not exactly sure how this thing spreads. The only thing we've got to our advantage right now is the first mutation. Since you're a confirmed carrier of it, I want you out here spreading the immunity to as many people as you can."

They busied themselves disinfecting the outer treatment area while they waited for the XO. It seemed the doctor's tone impressed how drastic the situation was, because they didn't have to wait long. Since there wasn't anyone else in the clinic, they explained what had happened over the empty space where the exam table had been positioned.

"How is this possible?" Kolpos stared at the geneticist.

"All life in the galaxy is based on the same DNA. It seems amino acids are as old as space-time itself and has been spread everywhere by the currents of dark energy."

Kolpos eyes grew large. "You mean to tell me that the fur-covered beast lumbering across the land has the same blueprint we do?"

The geneticist nodded. "Because of that, I was able to use our own genes to put the final touches on the virions."

"Making the mutations able to infect us." The doctor summarized.

The commander turned to Alhia. "You have a way to test this?"

The scientist had been staring at the floor seams. He looked up. "Yes."

"I don't want everyone traipsing through here seeing the captain stretched out." The commander pointed to the monitor on the wall. "I'm going to send out an order for everyone on board to report to your lab. Everyone with the second mutation gets sent here, even if they're not feeling sick yet. I don't want a ship-wide panic, so not a word of what this is about."

Velifer swam over with a sample kit. "You first."

The XO nodded as he held out an arm. "And you second."

Alhia was grateful the military officers were able to think logically about what needed to be done next. His own brain was too overcome with guilt to think rationally. As easy as it would be to lock himself in the isolation chamber to be a nursemaid for the C.O., he had clear orders and was needed more elsewhere for the time being. Once the specimens were collected, Kolpos headed towards the exit.

"Where are you headed now?" The doctor asked.

With one last look at the screen and the unconscious man lying on the other side of a sealed hatch, he answered. "To take command of the Catenata."

Alhia gathered up the samples and mentally prepared to repeat the nightmare he'd already been living through for days. It was time to find out the magnitude of the disaster he had created.

"I'll send Gomesi over to help you when he reports for his shift."

The scientist was surprised by the offer. He almost declined it, but then realized testing everyone in the crew would be more than he could do on his own. So instead he nodded. "Thank you."

Chapter Eighteen

After undogging the hatch, Alhia pushed the metal door back to its normal position. The room was already stale. It was a taste he was unaccustomed to and normally would find unpleasant. Still, he wanted to lock himself inside, but unfortunately, he needed to run the tests. That meant he needed to let everyone else on the crew into his private space. But his discomfort was no longer a consideration, not when lives were on the line.

The familiar steps of preparing the machines calmed him down. He had to focus his thoughts on what was in his hands and to block out the memories of the captain and Sauries laying in medical. Not allowing his mind to wander helped him get through processing the samples he had.

The results brought him both comfort and concern. Kolpos was positive for the first mutation. He would be immune to the lethal version. The doctor was negative for either. Alhia hoped that was still the case after treating the CO. Protocol called for him to relay the information to the XO first, but the acting commanding officer could wait. The doctor might not be able to. So he sent a secure private message to medical, then another to the Commander's suite, after which he filed away the results. When he turned around, the engineering master chief came through the door.

"Why aren't you out swimming?"

"I had to do some routine maintenance on the generators. There was an announcement for all hands to report here." The master chief looked around the lab. "Is this the right spot?"

"Yes." The geneticist ushered him into the room and motioned for him to wait. "Thank you for responding so promptly."

Alhia gathered his supplies for collecting specimens and hoped the career military man didn't notice that the equipment was designed to be used on animals. When the scientist turned around, the engineer was waiting for him next to the work bench. He set the magnetized instruments down where they stuck to the bench and made a silent wish that the corpsman would get there soon to assist him. While he was capable of getting the samples from people, it was still something he was not comfortable with. Then he plastered a smile on his face so the patient would not see that he was nervous and grabbed a dermal antiseptic.

"The instructions were for everyone on board to report here for testing. There are very few on board right now."

"We are aware of that. We will make sure everyone is accounted for."

He was relieved not to be pestered with questions. Well, at least not inquiries about what the tests were for. It was obvious the dark-mantled man with nine chevrons taking up most his upper arm had spent a lot of time thinking about the most efficient ways to complete a mission. Even being pulled from his normal environment and place into a strange setting, his mind still anticipated the needs of the command and what he could do to ensure everything was completed.

The scientist paused with the needle about to puncture the enlisted man's skin. He closed his eyes, then realized the other man was probably watching what he had just done and wouldn't want to have a medical procedure done by someone not looking at what they were doing. Not even a simple one like this. He opened his eyes and forced himself not to check whether the engineer was staring. He needed to portray confidence, even if he didn't actually feel it. He gulped down a large swallow of water and stuck the syringe into the vein.

The vial quickly filled up with enough blood to conduct the test. He withdrew the needle and applied the clotting agent. When he was sure the site wouldn't weep, he turned to the equipment he had just turned off. He powered everything back up and inserted the specimen.

"Is that everything?"

"Um, no." The geneticist talked over his shoulder without turning around to face the other man. "It will just take a few minutes to get the results. Then you can be on your way."

Diopus quietly watched everything that happened. Both men were comfortable in the silence, so neither spoke. Alhia didn't want to idly wait while the results were processed, so he sterilized the equipment he had used. By the time his chores were done, the chime indicated his wait was over.

"Is everything good?"

Alhia read over the results, and was relieved to see none of the DNA markers he was looking for. The head engineer hadn't been exposed to either mutation.

"Yes. Thank you."

The scientist gave a curt nod and made eye contact with Diopus. He even grinned. It was a genuine smile that rarely adorned his face. The master chief nodded in response, then turned to swim out into the passageway. As Diopus left, Gomesi came in. The petty officer yielded to the senior enlisted and let him go through the hatch first.

"Velifer told me to report here for my shift."

The petty officer's eyes darted about the room. He stayed near the door, hesitant to come all the way in. He looked unsure of the orders he been given and whether he should follow them. In his hands were the medical supplies designed to be used on their species, what the crewmen would expect to see when they came in. Alhia was grateful the other had brought the instruments with him. He took the kit and motioned for the other man to go to the bench.

"I will show you the process as I run the test on you, then we will divide the work. You can get samples, and I will run the machines."

The medical assistant nodded and got into place. He maintained the position of attention, and watched as his blood was collected. He stayed close and paid attention to how the specimens were prepped for analysis. Then he got to see how his DNA strands were entered into the machine for examination.

The scientist thought that the younger crewman would have questions, but none were raised. Then he realized the corpsman probably took samples and ran analyses on them routinely. There might be some slight difference with the change in equipment, but for the most part, it was all things he knew how to do.

"Everyone on board is going to need to be tested. The only ones that have been tested so far are the doctor, the X.O., myself and Diopus."

"And the Captain and Sauries?"

The geneticist had turned away to stow the gear that was no longer needed and turned back in surprise. Alhia wasn't sure what had been said to him, but Gomesi seemed to have a clear understanding of the situation.

"Yes. Them too. Everyone that is on board has been told to come here."

"And the people out swimming?"

"I'm sure that is being addressed as we speak."

Gomesi held up a portable screen he had brought with him. On it was a list of everyone on board.

"So we make sure no one gets overlooked. Do I just put a check next to the name when they complete the test?"

Alhia swam over to look at the screen. "Is there a way to put a notation instead of just confirmation?"

"Sure."

Alhia went back over the list of everyone he'd screened, instructing the junior enlisted man to put an "M1" next to anyone that had the first mutation, an "M2" next Sauries and Yosheia, and an "N" next to the two so far that showed no sign of foreign DNA.

A chime filled the room just as they finished. The scientist cringed when he saw the markers appear on the screen, but relaxed when it turned out to be the first mutation. Any further conversation was interrupted by the arrival of Kolpos and Ophis.

"I found this young man doing his rounds."

"I heard the announcement, but assumed you meant for me to report here after I'd been relieved." The seaman with only three white chevrons looked down sheepishly.

Gomesi went to work, not showing any of the apprehension the geneticist had at puncturing the skin of a fellow crewmember. All four of them made idle chatter as they waited for the test to complete, not giving away the reason for them all to be there.

Alhia frowned when the findings came in. Kolpos was there, looking over his shoulder. Alhia closed his eyes and hung his head.

"Is that…?" The commander quietly asked.

The geneticist nodded in response.

"Corpsman, Ophis needs to go directly to medical and straight into quarantine."

"Yes, commander."

The young male looked confused as he turned to follow the petty officer. "What does it mean, that I need to go into quarantine?"

"It just means that until he completely understands what's going on here, we're going to separate you from the rest of the crew. Don't worry. You won't be alone. The CO is already there."

"The CO?" His eyes widened. "Now I'm more afraid than I was of getting sick. I can't be alone with the ship's captain. What if I say the wrong thing?"

"Don't worry about it. He's really a nice guy."

They turned and went down the passageway, out of earshot.

The officer turned to Alhia. "I've secured all access points to the ship. I need you to relocate all needed equipment to the port entrance, and test everyone as they return. I did not send out a recall signal, so you would not be overwhelmed. The last thing I want is people mingling and exchanging scuttlebutt at the testing station."

"I will only detain them long enough to get the sample and confirm the results. Once they are confirmed negative, they will be sent on their way."

The acting CO turned with a concerned expression. "I don't need to tell you how important it is to keep this just between us."

"No." Alhia looked down, suddenly feeling guilty and unable to bear the weight of his gaze.

***

At first glance the alcyonacea looked like a wall, until Gomesi swam through the soft coral fans. Alhia knew going through the layers of membranes felt like being licked. The simple, flexible organisms consumed any small foreign bodies coming into the ship.

The scientist secured his equipment to the bulkhead, locking it into place. He felt a surge in the current when the outer hatch was opened. Then there was another voice.

"I heard that this was the only access point. When it was secured, I thought maybe I told the wrong information." Anale came through the coral curtain, surprised by the sudden change to the corridor.

"You have the right place." The corpsman reassured him. "We just need to do a quick test, then you'll be on your way."

"What kind of test."

"Just a scan of your DNA." Gomesi motioned to Anale's elbow.

He presented his arm and its seven white chevrons. The chief gave a look of surprise, but didn't interfere with his samples being collected. "With all my deployments, I've seen some extreme security measures, but I've never had to go through DNA identification to get back on a ship before."

All the machines were warmed up and ready for a specimen to be inserted. Alhia took the samples from the corpsman and used the opportunity to respond to the chief. "There is a first time for everything."

Curiosity made him take the couple extra seconds to watch for a reaction. Seeing the total look of surprise with the chief's mouth hanging open was worth it. Thankfully, the corpsman recovered quickly and resumed collecting the sample.

The chief looked confused. He obviously expected them to refute his assumption. There was an awkward silence as everyone waited for the results. Any time Anale looked like he was going to say something, the geneticist would smile and the chief would close his mouth. It seemed like he was trying to figure out the right response, but seeing the civilian grin made him second-guess himself. The machine chimed, and Gomesi and Alhia turned to see the results. The corpsman let the civilian share the news.

"Great news. We have one hundred percent certainty that you are who you claim to be."

The chief chuckled, and then stopped when no one else laughed with him. He eyes grew large, but still didn't speak up. He back away slowly, as if he expected to be stopped. When he wasn't, he eventually turned and swam away.

The petty officer was already preparing his equipment for the next person. When it was just the two of them, and no could over hear, he said. "I was not expecting that comment."

"Neither was Anale."

The enlisted man turned to face who he was talking to. "Is that why you said it?"

"Yes." When the other man didn't break eye contact, he continued. "It's very important not to spread fear among the crew until we know exactly what's going on."

Gomesi nodded and turned back to the syringe he was cleaning. The conversation wrapped up just in time. Halis was the next one in, with Eqmontis on her heels.

"What's going on?"

"It's just a quick test, and then you can be on your way."

The culinary specialist looked around with wonder while the guy next to her had a look of skepticism. Since she was the first through the doorway, Gomesi approached her with the sample kit. Anyone in the military was familiar with needles, so she exposed the interior of her arm. The corpsman smiled at her before turning his full attention to the task he was performing.

"I bet we've been exposed to radiation poisoning." the machinist declared with an authoritative tone.

Alhia rolled his eyes. "This solar system has a yellow dwarf sun, so the chances of that kind of exposure are minimal."

The culinary specialist didn't seem to hear any of the logical rebuttal. She looked down at her arm to confirm the small red puncture site wasn't bleeding, then turned to her shipmate with six black chevrons. "Have you seen cases of it?"

"No, but that's because I work in the engineering compartment. We have thick walls protecting us from atmospheric radiation." He gave the female a self-confident look, then moved into the spot she had just been taking up.

Halis absorbed every word he said, nodding along and encouraging him to continue. The corpsman gave the first set of samples to the scientist, and then turned back to the patients. He shook his head at the discourse.

"My medical training taught us there is very little chance of ionizing radiation even in systems with suns much larger than this one. The top layer of water molecules absorbs the high frequency waves, so everything in the water is safe."

He stuck the syringe without the concern for minimizing pain he normally had. The patient didn't seem to notice.

"But what about the people that went on the surface?" The engineer turned to Alhia as he spoke.

The scientist had just finished inserting the first set of samples for analysis. He turned back to face the conversation. "I'm right here, and I'm not sick."

Eqmontis leaned over to the female at his side. "He is here, but you notice that Sauries isn't. I heard she was taken to medical."

Gomesi slapped the clotting agent on as he pulled the needle out and rushed the test tube to the geneticist. He hoped for quick results, just so he wouldn't have to listen anymore of their theories.

"I heard that, too." Halis nodded up at him with wide eyes.

Alhia had his back to the people speaking. He closed his eyes and forced himself to relax. As much as he wanted to refute what was being said, it was in his best interest to say nothing at all. He couldn't tell them what was happening, so disputing his assumptions would just lead to more questions that the geneticist was not in a position to answer. Thankfully he was saved from having to speak by both of them being found uncontaminated.

"Your tests are clear. You can go."

"Did you notice he didn't say what the test was clear of? He doesn't want to admit that I'm right."

They both swam away, with Halis's whole head bouncing up and down as she nodded along with him and encouraged him to say more. Gomesi gave Alhia a puzzled look but wasn't given a chance to say anything. Teres swam up with a confused look.

"What's going on?"

"We just need to take a sample from you and run a quick test." The corpsman was already prepping the puncture site.

"All right."

He was quiet during his wait, seeming to be preoccupied with some other thoughts. Alhia wished all the subjects would be like him. Then the first scene displayed the markers. A knot formed in Alhia stomach. Now it was a fifty-fifty shot whether he was immune or sick. The second machine popped up confirmation of the latter.

"He's going to need to go to medical." The scientist faced the corpsman. "To the same area you took Ophis."

It was easier to not say it. He didn't want to admit that another crewman was being forced into isolation; that someone else was going to go through the same misery Sauries had the last few days of her life. The smile faded from Gomesi's face, he nodded, and he then turned and escorted the petty officer away.

Alhia leaned against the bulkhead, suddenly feeling the weight of the world on his shoulders. He didn't know if he could go through with this. Then someone else returned from their swim. He didn't have any other choice than to push through, complete the testing and find out just how serious the situation was.

He didn't know how tense he was until the results were negative, and his shoulders dropped down when he relaxed. He realized he hadn't said anything, so concluded with; "Thank you for your time. This data will help us with our research."

The crewman smiled, glad he could be of assistance, and swam away. Alhia watched as he disappeared around the corner. Then Gomesi was in his place, with a food container in each hand. Having nutrients and a series of clear findings helped Alhia calm down and be a little less apprehensive about what they were doing.

There was a long break between people. Both of them were content to remain silent. They had to find enough idle chatter when they had people to test, and both were relieved to not have to engage in it when no one else was around.

The quiet was interrupted by a peculiar noise. It wasn't until the sound repeated that Alhia recognized what it was. His assistant had fallen asleep. The guttural whisper was common when the body was completely relaxed. He smiled and let the other man rest.

"What?" Gomesi asked later. "Why did you let me sleep?"

"Because you needed to rest. Only one person came in, and I was able to handle it."

"Thank you." The petty officer bowed his head down.

Then it was the geneticist's turn to wake up disoriented. It took him a moment to realize where he was and remember why they were there. "Why didn't you wake me?"

"Because no one has come in. I figure only one of us needs to be awake to make sure no one slips by without being tested. We don't know how long this will take, so we might as well rest in shifts.

They had checked off everyone on the crew except Tarpon. Since no command had been issued to recall people back to the ship, they had no idea when he would return. They both sat and waited. After a while, Gomesi interrupted the silence.

"So I saw that my results were positive. Does this mean I'm going to develop symptoms later?"

The scientist was shocked at the question. He had assumed that the corpsman understood the situation. He had a sudden new respect for the man that went above and beyond his job requirements, all the while under the impression he would eventually die of the same illness he was treating.

"No, your results are the same as mine. We are immune to the version that causes the drastic symptoms you've seen."

Completely uncharacteristic of him, Alhia started talking. He explained to the petty officer everything he had found, then stressed the necessity for them to maintain patient confidentiality. It felt good to talk about what had happened and what he had done. He wasn't sure how this was all going to end, but he knew that he would never be able to pretend it hadn't happened.

"Do you think its possible Tarpon might have slipped onto the ship without us knowing about it?"

"Or been here before this all started and just didn't respond to the order?"

Gomesi was suddenly in position to leave. "It's a possibility. I will go to his quarters and inquire if anyone else has seen him."

When the corpsman returned, he had a downcast expression. "He is nowhere to be found on the ship, and no one has seen him."

The scientist nodded. "I will handle this."

He sent out a signal to the command suite. Soon after, the acting CO swam down to see them.

"What's the situation?"

"Everyone has been tested except one crewman. No one has seen him and he is not on board."

The commander nodded. "Very well. Seal up this hatch and take the submersed shuttle to go look for him. We can't have you waiting here when we have no idea when he's going to be back. He might be at the other end of the sea, for all we know."

Alhia remembered how beautiful the depths at the far end had been. It was the last time he had been happy. He hoped he didn't have to go back there for this.

Chapter Nineteen

The equipment was detached from the bulkhead. Alhia was going to tell Gomesi that he could handle the search on his own, but they both had a full armload as they made their way to the submarine two decks below them. The interior was smaller than the aircraft, but the cockpits were very similar. He thought of instructing the enlisted man to return to medical, but something kept him from speaking up, so they both climbed into seats with steering controls.

"Where do we even start?" The corpsman looked overwhelmed as he stared out at the vast expanse of water in front of them.

"Take us west, since that's the most popular route." The scientist motioned for the other man to take the controls. "I'm going to set up the scanners to extend to their maximum distance and only alert us to life forms the size we are looking for."

The younger man was accustomed to taking orders, and once again looked determined as he prepared to launch. It took a while to scroll through all the settings and get the sonar programmed. By the time Alhia looked up, they were clear of the ship. Gomesi had been glancing over to see if he was done. Their eyes met briefly, and then they both looked at the display screen. Neither of them spoke; they were both listening for the beep indicating the machine had found what they were looking for.

Time passed in silence. Their gaze met again. One looked tired, and the other weary.

"I'll set up a spiral search pattern." Alhia punched the commands into the console.

The small ship turned, carrying them in circles around the Catenata. The sea that had seemed so small when they set up the bio net and moved behind it suddenly appeared huge. How were they going to find one person in the whole body of water?

Soon their arc widened out, so they no longer felt like they were traveling in a circle. It turned out, Tarpon was to the west. They found him laying still in the water.

"That's not good." The corpsman stared at the screen.

"What?"

"He's not moving, which means water is not running over his gills." Gomesi looked down at the control panel. "At least there is some current here. That should keep some water circulating."

The medical technician got up, ran to the back and opened the rear hatch. Alhia maneuvered the submarine so they would be able to pull the sick crewman directly inside. By the time he made it to the back, Gomesi had the other man aboard. It was a huge relief to see Tarpon's eyes open.

The storekeeper struggled to get the words out. Gomesi fitted him with a mask that sent water with high concentrations of oxygen over his gills. Once that was in place, the patient was able to get out multiple syllables at a time.

"Don't know… what happened."

"It's okay. Just relax. We'll get you back to sick bay." Alhia turned to the corpsman. "Is there anything I can help you with?"

"Not back here." The petty officer motioned to the cockpit. "Just get us back as fast as you can. All I can do is keep him oxygenated and keep the blood circulating."

The scientist stood with his mouth open. It was a very simplistic way to state what needed to be done, yet completely accurate. All he could hope for was to keep the patient alive, who appeared to be losing consciousness. He rushed to the forward cabin, and shoved the throttle as far as it would go.

"There are emergency docking clamps at medical. Take us to those."

"Okay. How's it going back there?"

"I'm getting jostled around quite a bit back here, but since I don't think you're going to become a full-time medevac pilot, it's probably good enough."

Alhia had expected praise for how fast he made the return trip and was taken aback at the criticism. He slowed down, being gentle with the controls as he backed up to the larger ship.

"There is going to be a bump. We are clamping in."

"Thanks. One hand to steady me, the other one for the patient."

The emergency stretcher was already extended. The form laying on top of it was in and out of consciousness, completely unaware of what was going on around him. It felt weird coming into medical from the back side. Velifer looked up but didn't look surprised. Kolpos jumped back, startled by their coming through the hatch. Everyone's attention was immediately drawn to the stretcher.

"So he's positive?" The commander recovered from his shock and came forward.

The men guiding the unconscious patient looked at each other. "We never tested him. He was like this when we found him, so we started treatment and rushed him back here."

The doctor turned to open the hatch leading to the isolation ward, but the acting C.O was there ahead of him.

"I've got this. You stay back."

Alhia pushed the gurney into the next room, looking at the man holding the door for them. "I'm surprised to see you here."

"Well, I know I'm immune. The doctor is not. Having him treat the patients is a death sentence. I had you run off so fast that I didn't get the list of test results, so I don't know who else is immune. I'm not going to risk assigning this job to someone else when I know I can do it without endangering my life."

"The corpsman and I are both have the first mutation and we can take turns helping out in here. You can resume your responsibilities in command."

"Yes. I have a worried crew and all sorts of scuttlebutt flying around. It's time I go address them."

The door sealed behind them, then they went through the next one. Yosheia was stretched out on the closest platform. His eyes were shut and the only movement was a fluttering of his gills. Ophis and Teres were huddled together in the corner. At least they appeared to still be doing well. They transferred Tarpon to the next bed. Gomesi went to work getting the newest patient connected to the monitor.

Alhia turned to the screen. "Hey doc, I see the captain's I.V. is barely dripping. Do you want me to open it up a little bit?"

"No. After Sauries retained so much fluids, I'm trying a different approach with him."

"Well, do."

Velifer made a list of orders which appeared on the screen at the foot of the second bed. Gomesi started an I.V. and administered the medications. When the last item on the list had initials next to it, he closed his eyes and floated above the bed.

"Go to your berthing area and get some rest."

"What about you?"

"I caught a long nap hanging out in the passageway. You know, you watched me sleep."

The corpsman laughed. "Yeah, I did."

"So it's your turn."

Gomesi nodded and took one last look around. When he confirmed that everything had been put away, he turned to the door. "All right. You can rest when I get back."

With two patients unresponsive and the other two whispering in the corner, it was very quiet. Yosheia's fever spiked, so a cooling blanket was put over him. Even though he didn't have the severe pneumonia Sauries had experienced, he still had all the other symptoms. There wasn't much hope that the change in treatment was going to save him, so just like Alhia had the last time he had been locked in this room, he went from one task to another, taking care of the people who couldn't take care of themselves.

Velifer came on the screen. "I've been doing research and I've found another medicine I want you to try. I'm passing it through. Give it to Ophis and Teres first, since they have the highest chance of survival."

Alhia nodded at the camera, then went over by the door. The light above the pass-through indicated it was safe to be opened on his end. Inside were four syringes with the same dose in each.

The two in the corner that had appeared oblivious to their surroundings were now staring at what had just arrived. "That's going to help us?"

"We believe so. The doctor's been working non-stop out there to research similar cases in the medical database, reading what they tried for treatment and what success they had. We are all working tirelessly to keep you from going through—" Alhia motioned to the prone forms behind him, "—that."

They both swam forward. An antiseptic wipe was passed over the bulk of Ophis' shoulder muscle, and then the needle was inserted. The geneticist remembered how reluctant he had been to pierce Sauries' skin. Now he was giving injections without a second thought. When Teres' shot was complete, they both went back to the far side of the room. But instead of turning their back on everything they had like before, they stayed alert to what was going on around them.

Alhia had just finished giving Tarpon his injection when the sealed hatched opened. Gomesi came in and then closed it behind him.

"What can I do?"

"Nothing. I just have to dose the captain with this new medication and then everything will be done."

The corpsman swam over with his hand out. "I can do that."

"No need." He cleaned a spot on the thick muscles of Yosheia's backside and stuck the needle in. "I've got it."

"You can take a break now."

"In a minute. I need to make sure there isn't an adverse reaction to the drug."

Gomesi chuckled. "I could do that. I have some experience with that."

The older man sighed, "I know. I'll take a break in a few minutes."

They both went about doing the duties of one person, which meant they spent a lot of time waiting around for a change in the patient's condition or for it to be time to administer another dose to someone.

"Oh, wow." Miliaris' image was on the screen along with her voice. "It's worse than I heard."

Alhia was annoyed at the interruption, but went to stand in front of the camera. "What can we do for you?"

The female scientist grinned. "I came here to see if there was anything I can do for you. I know the tests didn't reveal anything. I can run them again if you have more samples. This time, we might be able to determine the cause."

The geneticist frowned even harder than he already had been. "We already found the cause. It's a mutation that's changed their DNA."

Miliaris' jaw dropped, her arms hung limply at her side, and her face lost all color. For the first time ever, she looked worried. "Well. None of my equipment will be of any assistance."

Gomesi swam up to also be on camera. "We appreciate the offer to help."

"Even though it appears that I can do no such thing."

The corpsman responded. "It still means something that you wanted to try."

There was another long stretch of silence, without even the murmur they had become accustomed to in the corner. Both those patients had fallen asleep. The blare of an alarm rang out in the room. Yosheia's heart rate had dropped to nothing, which caused his blood pressure and oxygen levels to also plummet. The corpsman rushed over and started artificial respiration and applied a cardiac stimulant.

"What can we do?" Alhia asked the screen.

The doctor's eyes were sullen when he answered, "Nothing. Anything we can do is intended to keep the patient alive until we can fix the underlying problem. Unfortunately, there is nothing else we can do. The only option we have now is to make sure he's not in pain.

Gomesi nodded and administered a syringe he had close by. He muted the alarm, but the screen still flashed. They watched as the numbers all fell to zero. When the monitors showed that all breathing and circulation had stopped, he turned the monitor off. He then went over to the cabinet and got out a bag to seal the body in.

Alhia helped zip the captain away and moved him into the make-shift morgue. A lump formed in his throat when he looked at the body bag already there. Then, he turned around and saw the two young men in the corner with their mouths wide open. There was a tremor in his hands. He turned and headed towards the exit. Gomesi looked up at he went by.

“I need a few minutes,” was all the explanation he offered before going through the decontamination process and leaving medical.

He didn’t look up. He didn’t notice if he passed anyone. He went to the only place he considered safe, his lab. Even there, he didn’t do anything. He crawled into his hammock and stared at the wall until movement at the door drew his attention. Kolpos entered.

“I know. I need to get back to work. I just need a few minutes to clear my head.”

“That’s not why I’m here.”

The scientist got out of his sleeping rack.

“Relax. I just wanted you to know that I’ve started preparations for launch. We are giving up on this mission and heading home.”

Alhia’s eyes were huge.

“I’ve wanted to do this for a long time, but it was never my call to make. Now I’m the one responsible for the crew, and I’m not waiting around for anything else to go wrong.”

“I can’t go back.”

The scientist couldn’t make eye contact. In fact, he couldn’t focus on any one thing. He felt trapped and had an irrational need to flee.

“I was worried that you would feel that way.”

He met the officer’s gaze. “I killed my own crewmates. I should feel that way.”

“Your tests were approved by the captain.”

The calm, sympathetic expression on the commander’s face irritated Alhia. There was no way to rationalize what had happened, and he couldn’t believe the military officer was doing just that.

“You know as well as I do, he had no clue what he agreed to.”

“That is something we will never know for sure.” Kolpos dipped his head. “I’ve been reading the logbooks from the biologist. They panicked over something they themselves had no part in creating and let that reaction drive them to suicide. You could have followed their example. When you saw the test results, you could have taken off for the first shark or pod of orcas you could find.

"Instead you stayed here. You helped us test the whole crew. Your experience operating the machines expedited the process much faster than anyone else could have. Your actions minimized the amount of people suffering from this. Now, you stay at the bedside of the people that are sick. While it upsets me that this has happened, your response to it has impressed me."

Alhia was silent. He felt like everything he had done was inadequate, like he'd never be able to do enough. "Thank you for saying that. But I don't think I can go back and face my family, knowing what I've done."

Kolpos gave a nod, confirming he heard what the other man had said.

Chapter Twenty

When Alhia woke up, it was the middle of the night. He hadn't expected to sleep that long, but it was probably for the best. The galley was empty, so he took two servings of algae and then grabbed two more, just in case Ophis or Teres were hungry. Sleep had helped. He didn't feel quite as overwhelmed as he had leaving isolation. The commander's words also made feel like his efforts hadn't all been in vain.

He made his way down the hall. The lights were in on medical, and Velifer was leaning over a screen. He looked up and nodded when the other man entered.

"Tarpon passed away while you were resting."

The scientist closed his eyes. The guilt of causing another death swept over him. But there was also a little relief that he hadn't had to witness it. "I guess I should get back in there and see what I can so to assist the other two."

"Before you do," Velifer motioned over to what he had been reading, "I was wondering if you would take a look at this. It's some really old case files and their treatment notes. Unfortunately, they don't use medical abbreviations, so they're rather long. I get the impression this care was given by scientists instead of medical doctors, so you might have better insight than I do as to why they chose the options they did and if something similar would work for us."

Alhia started reading over the officer's shoulder. He was right, it did read like a research log book instead of a patient chart, though it was obvious they were trying to save the man's life. He nudged forward until he was directly over the screen.

Hours went by as the scientist devoured the information in front of him. He forgot all about the food he had brought and failed to notice when the doctor passed it on to the people confined in quarantine.

"Of course, that's it!" Alhia called out.

The physician had been snoozing in the corner and was startled away. With his eyes still blinking to adjust to the light he asked, "You found a cure?"

"No." The geneticist wilted, but only slightly. "But I might have found a way to keep them alive until they're back on the home world."

"How?"

"We need to flood their bodies with phosphates. The genes I created attach to the outside of a cell at the phosphate receptor. If we saturate all the receptors so they are all full of phosphates, then the virions will not have an attachment point available. They won't be able to get into the cell. It could slow the infection long enough to get them to the hospital. How much phosphate do you have?"

"Quite a bit actually, if you consider all the medications it's in. In fact, it was one of the main ingredients in the drug you injected into them last night."

"Good." The scientist swam around in circles, mimicking the thoughts swirling around in his brain. "Then we can already see if that dose has slowed the rate of symptom progression and can increase it if it hasn't."

They both swam over to the monitor, and waved to get the other people's attention. Gomesi saw the gesture, and came over to be directly in front of the camera. They could see the two patients were despondent in the corner. It was good to see that neither of them were lying on a gurney, but they had hoped the patients would look better than they had before the treatment.

"How's it going?" Velifer asked.

"Both of them ate. Their vitals are steady. Physically, they are doing fine."

"Ophis, Teres, can you come over here? We have something to share with you."

They both turned towards the screen.

"You found a cure?" the petty officer asked.

"Well, not exactly." The doctor turned to the civilian next to him. "Why don't you explain?"

Alhia cleared his throat, then finally looked up at the image in front of him. "I don't want to get your hopes up."

"I don't think there is anywhere for our hopes to go but up. We are trapped in a cell waiting to die a slow painful death." It seemed the higher ranking of the two patients had become the spokesman for both of them. The seaman peeked over his shoulder.

"Well, what I meant is I don't want your expectations to be set too high. You'll still have to stay in quarantine until you make it back to one of the primary worlds. We don't have a way to cure you, so you'll be contagious until you make it to a facility where they can."

"Primary world?" The seaman came forward. "You think we could live long enough to make it home?"

"How do you feel, right now?"

The two infected crewman looked at each other.

"Bored." Teres answered.

The scientist laughed. "They're bored."

"Hopefully, you'll feel that for a long, long time." The doctor added with a smile.

"Excuse me for my outburst. After three patients that were struggling to breathe, it's a relief to hear you say you're bored," the geneticist explained.

"And we will find ways to alleviate that for you."

"Basically, we have found a medication that will slow the rate of infection so you can make it to a facility that can treat you. You'll have to stay in here until you get there."

"But we're going to live?" Ophis asked.

"That's the plan."

The two patients grabbed each other's arms and starting going around in circles. Even Gomesi was smiling as he prepared the room for long-term habitation.

The officer turned to Alhia. "I'll call Miliaris. I think she can extract that compound so we'll have fewer side effects to manage. Can you help her with that?"

"Unfortunately, no. I won't be making the trip back with you guys."

The doctor looked surprised, but didn't say anything. Instead he looked up and gave him a formal greeting. He understood being given that greeting at that time was a show of respect and gratitude. He bowed his head in response, not having the strength to inform the officer he was not worthy of either.

Once out in the passageway, Alhia was lost in his thoughts. When he swam away from the ship, he was going to head to the river and the strong currents Sauries had wanted to experience. Going there would honor her memory.

Turning right, he headed back to his lab. He wasn't sure why, but there wasn't anywhere else to go, so he went back to the only space that was his. Through the passageways, he could see preparations were already underway to launch.

He froze in the doorway to his lab. The room was bare. All of his equipment was gone. He crossed the threshold, wondering if this was his punishment for what he had done. Had all of his research been confiscated? Destroyed?

"Scientist Alhia, please report to the bridge. Alhia, you are needed on the bridge."

The ship-wide communication system was rarely used, and the announcement took him by surprise. He was grateful the message was repeated so he could confirm he had heard it correctly. He took one last look around the room, confirming there was nothing there, and made his way to the top of the ship.

The transition pool was bustling with activity. There was just enough room for him to sit on the edge and stretch. Everyone else was caught up in conversations about the impending launch. They didn't even seem to notice him.

When all of his rituals had been done, he stood up and walked down the corridor. The hatch to the engine room stood open. Everyone hurrying about had black chevrons on their arms. He didn't even slow down to see what was happening inside. Kolpos stood at the bottom of the ladder that went up to the bridge. Alhia was grateful he didn't have to climb the dreadful contraption again.

"Everyone seems very busy."

"Plans are to leave before dark. I figure there is no sense in staying here any longer than we have to."

"Thank you for notifying me before launch. I'll leave now."

"Before you go." The commander walked by and motioned for him to follow. The scientist wasn't sure where they were headed, and he had concerns that he might be kept from leaving. All those concerns dissipated when the officer turned and climbed into one of the shuttlecraft. He tentatively followed. He was surprised to see that all but the back row of seats had been taken out. In its place, the equipment from his lab had been set up. There was even an algae dispenser sat in the corner.

"Once we leave here, no one will ever return to this planet. I'm having the entire thing quarantined. If you want to stay here, I thought you could use a few comforts to make it easier and help protect you from the elements."

"But I thought," the scientist stammered. He turned full circle which ended with him looking at the acting CO with a shocked expression. "When I saw my lab was empty, I assumed I was being punished. This seems more like a reward."

Kolpos shrugged. "Being deserted on a planet labelled as uninhabitable seems like punishment enough. Beside, I'm grateful for the lives you saved."

"Commander." Diopus was in the doorway. "The engines are ready to fire. Should I start the pumps to drain the submerged portion?"

"Yes, master chief. Alert the crew to move to the area that will remain flooded for liftoff." The officer turned back to the scientist. "If you're going to leave, you have to do it now. We are ahead of schedule, and you need to get clear of the launch area."

"Thank you, commander." Alhia motioned to everything around him. "I appreciate all of this."

"I will have to notify the admiral that you have communications equipment, so if there's another ship in the area, they might try to talk with you, even if they can't land."

"I will keep the radio on."

"Well, don't worry too much about it. It will be a long time before they have another mission in this arm of the galaxy."

Kolpos put a hand on the other man's shoulder and held his gaze. Then he lowered his arm, turned around and left. Alhia climbed into the cockpit and the chair he had become quite familiar with. He went over the preflight check list. When that was complete, he slowly rose up from the Catenata. He circled around, taking one last look at his home for the last century. With a sigh, he turned north, and headed to the bays he knew would offer him protection.

The great ship slowly rose out of the sea as the pumps drained water out of the interior spaces, and the engines started to overtake gravity. As droplets still streamed down the sides as thrust was increased until a wall of wind and sea water blocked Alhia's view. Then, above the chaos, the silver ship with engine ports forcing air over the spiraling bottom half climbed into space.

Epilogue

"Hello." Alhia stopped what he had been doing to listen. It had been more than a lunar cycle since the Catenata had launched. There was no one left on the planet to talk to him, so it made no sense for him to hear words, let alone a greeting.

Then, he worried that something had happened to the ship. Maybe it was no longer spaceworthy? Maybe it was returning to the planet, and they were contacting him to let him know they were coming—though this theory did not make sense. The sound he heard was coming from the west, but his shuttle was to the south. A radio transmission was the only logical explanation for why he would hear voices. As if to confirm the sound was real, he heard it again.

"Hello." His head turned to the west, the direction the sound seemed to come from, but he didn't see anything. None of his senses picked up anything other than the noise. He turned the other way, and swam towards his shuttle.

The aircraft was sealed tight. He lowered the ramp and climbed inside. Just as he had expected it to be, the radio was turned off. He stood there for a moment just staring at it. If what he heard hadn't been coming from the Catenata, he had no idea how to explain it. Maybe the guilt of killing three crewman and two cows had finally drove him insane.

Before he admitted to having auditory hallucinations, he powered up the ship's computer. He waited for the scanner to sweep the vicinity. It immediately beeped, indicating there was something alive out there. He had to wait for the high-resolution scan and almost fell over when he saw the small dolphins jumping through the waves.

Suddenly he understood the funny accent on the end of the hello; it was said through an elongated mouth. He rarely dealt with the engineered animals, and had forgotten that they had rudimentary language skills. He slid into the co-pilot's seat he had been leaning against. He wasn't losing his mind; there was just a problem with the bio net.

The beep every time the system circled over the mammals was annoying. He turned it off, stood up and walked to the back. The ramp was still down, so he stepped out onto it and looked in the direction they were coming from—and they were coming.

The thought of having a conversation, even a very basic one, was an exciting prospect. The expectation that he would never talk to anyone again made the idea of even a simple dialogue very stirring.

He realized this meant he would have to repair the bio net. Then he would have to do another scan of the sea. If he did find any predators, he would have to take care of them. If he could get them near the surface, he could use the anti-gravity lift on the shuttle to carry them out to the ocean. As long as it wasn't an entire pod; that would be more of a challenge.

"Hello." His focus returned to the cresting waves around him. It was a pod that approached him, but the individual members were about his size, or smaller. Not nearly as intimidating as being surrounded by orcas. These carnivores weren't even as fearsome as the canines he had relocated away from his heard. While these mammals did work together, it wasn't to bring down bigger game. No matter how many dolphins were coming, he was relatively safe. Still, he activated the ship's defenses and stayed on the ramp.

The slick grey bodies breaking through the water's surface finally came into view. Their bodies were a much better design for the water than his own species that had evolved on land and then returned to the ocean. These animals didn't have adaptions for traversing continents. They had no arms or legs, just a streamlined form to propel them through the surf. In some ways, he was envious of them and their lack of appendages.

Though there was a reason why they had inferior intellect. His intelligence trapped in a body without any method of physical expression would be torture. He paled at the thought of a complete understanding of his species genome and being unable to operate even a basic microscope. He could imagine, with romantic ideals, that he would learn to appreciate that form, that he would develop curiosities within his physical abilities, but he was very grateful to have an array of machinery behind him and the hands to operate it.

His attention was, once again, brought back to the scene in front of him as he tried to figure out what it was he saw. One of the forms coming through the waves did not look like the others. It was similar in color and size, but did not reach the height the others did jumping. It could be that one of them was injured, or had some type of deformity that kept it from reaching peak efficiency. His eyes tracked back and forth, looking for a body almost identical to the others around it, other than one slight variation. Instead, it was a form almost identical to his that broke the surface.

"Hello." It seemed his auditory hallucination changed to match his visual one. This salutation did not have the slight mispronunciation at the end. It was the same as if he, Sauries, Yosheia, or any of the other voices echoing through his head had said it. Is this what the other scientists had felt like at the end, like their mind was tricking them?

"When I saw the Catenata had launched, I thought I'd been left all alone on this planet. I can't tell you how great it is to see you."

He felt the world spin and knew he was falling, but that was just a brief moment's realization of what was happening. He didn't have time to react. When he regained consciousness, he was sprawled across the ramp, much closer to the bottom edge than where he had been standing. He had heard of people on the surface blacking out when their blood pressure suddenly dropped and there was no longer the minimum pressure needed to maintain circulation to the skull. The brain doesn't have nutrition or oxygen reserves, so it quickly stops functioning. Thankfully, the condition seemed to correct itself once he was lying flat and his arteries didn't have to fight against gravity to keep blood flowing to his mind.

"Are you all right?"

Her grey face emerged from the water right in front of him. There was no longer any doubt that another member of his species, of his crew, had been left behind and was now stranded on the planet with him. She reached out to grab hold of the ramp.

"No. Stay back."

She jerked back in response, then gave him a confused expression.

"I've engaged the ship's defense systems. You'll get an electric shock if you touch the shuttle. Give me a moment to get my bearings and I'll turn it off."

At least she no longer looked alarmed as she treaded water. He recognized her as one of the scientists that had been part of his orientation group when he arrived on the Catenata, but he couldn't remember her name. He stood up, went to the control panel and powered down the hull defense.

"I thought I was the only one left on the planet. So seeing you was a bit of a surprise."

Her mouth fell open, her shoulders sagged below the water line, and gaze cast downward. "So they did leave without me. My submarine got the message I needed to return immediately for emergency departure. I packed up everything and headed back at full speed, but I was on the other side of the ocean. Then I got the message that it had launched."

He turned to her with eyes bulged. "Why didn't you radio them that you were on your way?"

"My submersed craft was attacked by a shark soon after I started my mission. Apparently it didn't taste very good, so he gave up trying to eat it. In the process on gnawing on it, though, he had damaged my transponder. I could receive communications, but I couldn't send any."

"They wouldn't have left if they'd known you were here." He solemnly replied. "Not until you were back, anyway. Most of the scientists on board were killed, so when you didn't report in, it was assumed you were one of the casualties."

Her head disappeared under the water. When it reappeared, she had built up momentum, and propelled herself onto the edge of the ramp, in a move very similar to what he did at the transition pool. He sat down beside her and let his feet dangle in the water.

"I'm the geologist. My orders were to map all the volcanic activity on this planet. If I had found anything that endangered the mission, I would have returned immediately, but nothing I saw made me concerned. I've charted the plates, highlighting the areas of frequent tectonic activity, and located the thin spots where magma is rising to the surface. I thought I had plenty of time to get back."

"You would have, if this had been a normal mission. We lost so many crewman, I can't keep track of all their names."

"I'm Swanii."

"What?" He looked at her with a frown.

""My name is Swanii. What is yours?"

He chuckled. Of course he had forgotten all about something as simple as introducing himself. "I'm Alhia."

She looked up at the bright blue sky above them. “So, was that why they left? The death count reached too high?”

“Not entirely.”

After that comment, she turned and gave him her full attention. He told her what had happened, from when they first moved to the sea until he fainted. She sat, listening to his every word. Her expression showed shock and grief for what they all had been through, but she never interrupted him. By the time he was done, he felt hollow inside.

“Did you say cheese?”

He jerked back in surprise. “Did you not hear what I said? I killed people. Our crewmembers. The milk, and this entire planet and irrevocably contaminated because of what I have done. All the milk and cheese were thrown out, because that was the source of the infection.”

“Actually, I did hear every word you said.” She calmly responded. “And I was upset when I saw that I had been left behind. But if I were to only have one planet to explore for the rest of my life, this is a pretty good one. There is life in every niche you can find. There are huge coral reefs, teeming with colorful fish. Then I find out I might have access to an aircraft to explore the continents and the geological activity above the water. And now I might have access to cheese.”

She put up her hand to stop him from interrupting her.

“You also said that you have the first mutation that makes you immune to the deadly one. Since I’m stuck here, I’m going to have to get me some of that, because if this thing is mutating as quickly as you make it sound, I’m going to get one of them either way. So, I’d rather have the one you have. Once I’m immune, there isn’t any reason not to enjoy cheese.”

He shook his head, unable to argue with her logic. They sat there for a moment in silence, listening to the waves lap against the ramp.

"How did you survive out there?"

She turned, flashed him a big smile, and then chirped. Moments later four dolphins popped their heads up out of the water.

"The orcas clearly are abnormally aggressive here, but the smaller dolphins do everything they are supposed to. They found me battered and a little dazed in the sub after the attack. They surrounded me, calling out to me until I came out. See, there is safety in numbers. And they've learned how to defend themselves against predators. Eventually I felt comfortable enough to program the shuttle to follow us, and I swam with the group."

He motioned out just as one dolphin did a back flip through the air. "So, you've been with this same group this whole time?"

"No." she shook her head. "One of the first things I learned was that this ocean is expanding. Other than that, there is not much going on, plate tectonic-wise. I needed to get to the other side of the world. To get there, I had to get close to the polar cap. Even in summer, they didn't want to get that close to the ice. So, I stayed in the sub until I got to the next ocean. There I found another pod that was just as friendly and just as protective. This is actually the third group I've been with."

"How do?" A male dolphin slid his upper body onto the ramp between them.

Alhia leaned back in surprise, then responded, "I am well. How are you?"

"Good. Good." The dolphin laughed and then slid back into the water.

"They are not the most articulate conversationalists, but it's a whole lot better than being alone on a foreign planet with predators behind every rock."

Sitting there looking at her, it dawned on him for the first time that this was the rest of his life. There were no more missions. He would not make any more trips back to the home world to visit his family. He didn't have anyone to answer to. At least now he had a reason to keep going. He would take her to every peak he could find, if it made up for what he had done.

The End.

About C.E. Chester

C. E. Chester is a Coast Guard veteran. She worked on ambulances and in an ER as a paramedic. She is currently writing her next novel in Montana, where she lives with her husband and the animals they've rescued.

Social Media

Facebook: facebook.com/c-e-chester-438433273356112

Email: cechesterbooks@gmail.com

Made in the USA
Columbia, SC
02 June 2021

38498651R00093